left astray

Nathan Ewbank

Illustrations by Guilherme Sousa

ISBN: 979-8-9885632-9-7

Dedicated to all cats around the world

and those who love them.

Chapter One

Dahlia

Dahlia gorged herself on the food her human provided. It was rare for her humans to provide such bounty and she wanted to finish it all before they changed their minds and decided to take some back. The grilled sardines were a far step above the dry kibble they'd been feeding her of late. They smelled of the sea, their rich oily flavor and moist flesh had her gobbling so quickly she nearly choked, oblivious to the soft litany of "I'm sorry, I'm sorry, I'm so sorry Dahlia" coming from her human.

She didn't even look up as her human moved back onto the boat they traveled on. Didn't notice as that boat began to move away from the quay they'd tied up to.

It wasn't until her belly was almost satiated that she looked up and noticed her home and her humans were far out on the water. Farther than she could reach by jumping. One of them, the one called Alice, sat with legs dangling over the side of the boat staring at her with water glistening on her cheeks.

Dahlia didn't know what to make of that. She wasn't worried though. She knew as soon as they realized they'd left her they would turn around and come back to pick her up. She was royalty after all, and they'd been touring her around the world on this pleasure boat as long as she could remember.

At any moment now, one of the deep voiced ones would call out and the boat would swing around and come back toward her.

Only it didn't.

They didn't.

Dahlia watched and waited as her boat and her humans shrank from her view, becoming a tiny dot on the horizon, and then, nothing.

Just nothing.

Her belly stirred, swollen and round with a pregnancy she was only partially aware of.

She looked around and realized she'd been staring out to sea for a very long time, her hunger was back and there were no humans about to provide her with a meal.

As realization began to set in, a voice sounded off from behind her.

"Oh scratch! Talk about a tough break. I feel for you, I really do. Humans are the worst, aren't they?"

Dahlia turned, startled by the intrusion. Her head dropped and her ears folded back immediately but she resisted the urge to make her body loom as large as possible.

Behind her sat two strays, one orange and white, the other with a hood darker in color. They seemed to be appraising her casually, but she couldn't for the life of her think of why they might be doing it. Still, the orange one had his ears forward and was looking right at her, she understood what that meant well enough.

"What did you just say?!" she spat at them.

The darker one leaned back a little bit, his ears going passive.

"Look, w-w-we don't w-w-want any…"

"I SAID, tough break." interrupted the orange one, still facing her aggressively. "Humans are the worst, amiright? Eh? What with them abandoning you like that and all."

"They didn't abandon me!" she hissed.

Her hunger was making her irritable, and she was about fed up with this orange adolescent challenging her. She yowled.

"I am your queen! Blessed of Bastet, who was goddess to all cats. See my spot! I have been touched by the goddess herself!"

She puffed forward to show her badge of pride while bristling, letting the orange cat know she wouldn't back down. The dark one shrank back from her but the orange one didn't move. He looked ready to accept her challenge.

Then something unexpected happened.

He laughed.

Laughed!

Long hearty meows of full-throated amusement, interspersed with stammered excerpts from the speech she'd just hit them with…

"Meowwowow, Blessed of Bastet? Mhahahaaha, my queen?! MINE?? Hmeeooowwwhahah! Touched By The Goddess? Meowwaaahahaaaa-haaaha! Oh scratch, that's rich!"

Somewhere in the distance a human voice called out, loud and angry, a reprimand. He calmed down a little bit at that, but quiet chuckles wracked his body as he licked a paw and ran it over the top of his head a few times.

"What's your name?" he asked.

"Dahlia"

"Well Dahlia, I'm Calix and this is Nyke" the barest flicker of his ears to indicate the darker colored cat behind him. "Though you wouldn't know it from his actions. Nyke, you make for terrible back up."

"S-s-sorry" Nyke said dryly.

"No matter." Calix said, turning his attention back to Dahlia.

"How about we go find something to eat whilst I explain the rules of Poros to you? You'll need to know them when the council finds out you've been abandoned here."

He looked at her seriously again, his ears coming forward slightly.

"You'd do well to keep all that stuff about royalty and goddesses to yourself."

Then he turned to follow Nyke, who'd already moved away.

All Dahlia heard was "eat". She gathered herself and followed as they sauntered off down the quay.

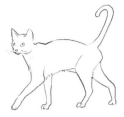

Chapter Two

Dahlia

CALIX'S STRIPED TAIL WEAVED up and down like a beacon beckoning her toward her next meal. He was talking but she couldn't really make out what he was saying. She was losing herself in a haze of worry at the movement she felt stirring in her belly, and thoughts of Alice's final kindness. To stave off the melancholy growing in her, she trotted up next to Calix to better hear what he was saying.

"... only a set number is allowed to forage along the quay where the fishermen and tourist humans hang out. The council chooses who can and can't and considers a multitude of factors in making those decisions. If you've got a human caring for you on the upper tiers, how adamantly you beg for scraps at the human feeding places, your overall appearance, things like that. You might actually get a spot, scratch you, seeing as you're about to have a bunch of young ones running around. Those touristy humans, they LOVE kittens, especially the...Hey, what's wrong with you?"

Dahlia had stopped cold, frozen, unable to move as a million fractured puzzle pieces joined together in her mind's eye and a wave of understanding swept through her. She'd known it, at an instinctual level she'd known it, but hadn't had the words for it. Those words, those scratch words. They were like a shout ringing in her ears, "young ones", and then the one that had clicked everything into place for her "kittens".

"*Kittens!*" the words flared in her mind.

"*I am pregnant,*" she thought to herself, "*Great mother Bastet, I'm pregnant!*"

Visions of other cats, swollen bellies swaying as they walked, swam to the fore in her mind and connected the dots to the current shape of her own body. She saw mother cats lying on their sides as an army of kittens pawed at them satiating their hunger for milk. Little ones nipping at tails, paws and ears, never giving a moment's respite. A memory of herself made itself known, that of her own mother and the comfort in feeling the prickly surface of her tongue methodically cleaning the top of Dahlia's head as she snuggled down to sleep. It filled her with longing and sorrow, then understanding, chased by rage.

"*This was why they abandoned me,*" she realized "*Bastet scratch them!*"

Her caretakers had betrayed the trust the goddess had placed upon them. In her greatest hour of need no less. They'd known, oh they'd known, the gutless spitters.

"*KITTENS!*"

Everything came back to her and aligned more clearly in her mind as she seethed. Lessons learned and bits of knowledge gleaned from others in passing came together. She understood what her time of odd moods was now, that it meant she was ready to mate. They'd almost always been out to sea when this time came so all that really came of it was her demanding extra attention from her humans. Oh, but that one time. She knew it now. Their ship was tied to a pier when the mood hit her. Her humans had been ashore somewhere, she'd called for them, yowled for their attention. Only they hadn't answered. She'd almost decided to go look for them when that big brute of a tom had jumped aboard and attacked her. It had felt like an attack anyway, at the time. The pain of him, lancing up her spine from behind her tail as his teeth gripped the loose skin at the nape of her neck. The recollection rolled through her memory, and she shuddered.

She understood now that he'd been mating with her. Knowledge and experience again merging in a spiteful union that felt like her own mind was mocking her.

"SCRATCHING KITTENS!" her mind screamed.

With Her inner rage boiling over, she wanted to go back and confront that tom. To rip his ears off! To rake his body with her claws! She wanted to scratch out the eyes of her humans, who'd abandoned her, rather than face the prospect of kittens on their boat. They cast her off like a broken piece of equipment, no longer useful. She wanted to curse Bastet for putting her in this position. A member of the royal line, reduced to nothing more than a stray about to mother to a brood of kittens

"TAIL PULLING KITTENS!", was the only thought she could form.

"Hey? Hey there? You alright Dahl?"

"M-m-maybe she was turned to s-s-stone."

Nyke's voice carried some of her anger away like a breeze, so gentle and full of compassion it was. Her eyes focused on the two of them and she blinked.

She opened her mouth to remind Calix that her name was Dahlia and not "Dahl" or "Dal" or "Lia" or whatever stupid nickname he tried to collar her with but,

"SCRATCHING KITTENS!", was all that came out.

Followed by an uncontainable scream of fury.

She paused and sucked in air, filling her lungs. A long tirade, the words lining up behind her tongue ready to lash out at any available target. All of her thoughts suddenly tangled up though, as a new voice interrupted the focus of her thoughts.

"It appears we have much to discuss then. Allow me to introduce myself, my name is Mikos, and I sit on the council here in Poros."

Dahlia was done, she didn't care anymore. Not about Calix, Nyke, her Humans, or this new cat Mikos. She was at the end of her patience.

"Well, "Mikos" she quipped,

Mikos began to open his mouth to speak and was cut off before a single mewl...

"Unless you've got some fish, I don't scratching care who you are, what your name is, or what council you sit on"

With that, Dahlia walked away, leaving the other three sitting there, staring at her dumbfounded.

She could not have cared less, there were some tables further along the quay that had humans sitting at them eating and she felt she needed some food too. Her belly gurgled as she made her way over to them.

Chapter Three

Dahlia

UNCERTAINTY CREPT UPON DAHLIA as she approached the humans. She'd never actually had to approach any humans, other than her own, to ask them for food.

She thought back to her first time, her mother, denying her and her sibling's milk. Sending them off and telling them all they had to fend for themselves from now on. They'd been scared. Approaching the humans warily, hiding in the shadows or under tables and chairs nearby waiting on some morsel to fall to the ground. Hoping to be fast enough to snatch it up before one of the others. She'd gotten tired of that REAL fast, realizing rather quickly that it was a losing strategy.

Besides, her mother had kept insisting that she and Dahlia were royalty, "Blessed of Bastet" as she put it. Why should she be hiding and fighting with her siblings over pieces of dirty scraps the humans hadn't wanted?

She'd made a decision to try something different, to demand the food that was hers by rights as a member of feline royalty.

To the amazement of her brothers and sisters, young Dahlia had trotted out from her hiding place, sat down next to and in full view of four humans having their breakfast, and demanded some of their food as loudly as she could.

The humans had stopped eating, looked down at her, and then burst into a chorus of laughter.

Dahlia had been ready to yell at them again when a piece of something appeared in the air as if from nowhere and landed on the ground right in front of her. A quick sniff had been enough to tell her it was food and she'd almost swallowed it whole in her excitement.

The next piece of food had landed a little closer to the humans, and she'd rushed over to it to snarf it down, but even as her teeth were sinking into that new bit of food a hand had grabbed her by the scruff of her neck and raised her into the air.

Dahlia had found herself suddenly and terrifyingly face to face with a human. She'd panicked and tried scrambling, twisting and turning, contorting her body in an attempt to free herself from the human's grasp. She'd hissed and spat her displeasure, loudly demanding to be let go, which had only made them laugh harder.

Her memory of events after that was a little foggy. She remembers they'd put her somewhere dark, where she ended up being jostled around quite a bit. She remembers a giant hand occasionally giving her food or caressing her.

Then the next thing she has a memory of was being on the boat and living on it as if that had always been her life. She briefly wondered where those in between memories had gotten to, but it didn't really matter. They'd taken good care of her, her humans, it had been a good life. Easy, relaxing, full of attention and food. She'd never wanted for anything.

Until they'd up and abandoned her, because she was going to have kittens.

"Tail Lickers!" she hissed

What this amounted to though is that the first humans Dahlia had ever approached had taken her as their own and cared for her. Nothing in her life thus far could have informed her just how lucky she'd been to have that be their reaction.

Now here she was, approaching another group of humans. She had no reason to believe these would treat her any differently. They were humans, why else did they exist, if not to serve?

Dahlia nonchalantly walked up, sat down next to the closest human and looked up at it expectantly, willing it to drop some food for her.

The human ignored her, all of them were ignoring her.

"I demand that you feed me." she said to them.

No reaction.

"I demand food, I am in need of sustenance!" she said louder.

One of the humans glanced toward her, looked at the others and said something. The others nodded, chuckling to themselves.

"Give me some foooooooood!" Dahlia wailed.

She moved toward the one who'd looked at her, fully intending to jump up in its lap and claim some food for herself.

One of the humans shouted sharply and in a blur of motion something large and rough caught Dahlia in the side knocking the breath out of her and sending her flying across the quay.

Pain like she'd never known arched through her body as her claws scrabbled at the concrete surface, trying to slow her movement.

She took one last glance at the humans. Then her body slipped over the edge, and she fell, cool sea water swallowing her whole.

Chapter Four

Mikos

MIKOS HAD WATCHED THE whole thing unfold and had known what was going down. There was no reason that he could think of for the human to have set the black cat ashore to feed a generous meal to it there.

Besides, he'd seen it happen before, all too frequently.

"Humans," he thought to himself, *"as Calix is so fond of saying, are the worst."*

A low rumbling purr came to life in his chest, signaling his distaste for those types of humans.

As the one on watch duty today it was his job to go down and see what was what and get everything figured out. Who this new stray was. What to do with her. From here she looked to be pregnant, but he couldn't be sure. That would open up a whole other brand of questioning and decisions. He wasn't sure the council would be all that happy with another stray showing, much less a stray about to drop a litter of kittens. Perhaps there was room in one of the farther settlements, or even across the mainland.

Mikos was about to jump down off his windowsill and head down to the quay when a voice called out.

His human was looking for him. He entertained the idea of ignoring them outright, but he'd done that a few times already this week and humans were kind of fickle, better to go see what the human wanted. After all, there could be some food in the deal. It was never a good idea to turn down food.

He jumped down and moved toward the sound of his human. She hemmed and hawed when she saw him, crouching down and extending a hand in his direction. Dutifully he went to her and arched his back, pushing against her open palm in that way that always felt so good. His tail rose straight up in pleasure at the attention, then shot right back down as she grabbed him, pulling him into her lap.

Then the brush came out. Mikos squirmed and tried to free himself, but she had him pinned down in a very practiced way. Thin metal tines began sifting through his fur, he actually enjoyed it, much to his chagrin. Still, one couldn't go around letting humans have their way, it set a bad example.

So, he put on a good show of struggling to free himself all while turning this way and that to ensure she got all the spots where his coat was starting to get matted and perhaps a little too thick. It was a love hate thing.

After an hour of that she finally let him go but then made the sounds that indicated she was about to feed him. He decided to hang around, it's not like the stray could go anywhere where they couldn't find her.

His human brought out some meat and began hand feeding it to him. He gently plucked each morsel from her fingertips, careful not to nip her flesh and disrupt her process.

Many morsels later Mikos lay down on his favorite pillow. Freshly brushed and fed he needed a nap. Kneading at his favorite pillow, Mikos thought of the stray again.

He'd get to it when he was done with his nap.

Besides, he knew Calix and Nyke were down there even though they weren't supposed to be. Calix with Nyke in tow would absolutely introduce herself to a new stray.

There was even a good chance Calix would educate the new one on all the rules and regulations of their community here. In the form of complaining about them sure, but at least she would be thorough.

"That's settled then" he said to himself as his eyes closed and sleep overtook him. "Calix can explain the rules, then I'll get in there and take care of the details."

With a yawn and a stretch, he drifted away to dreams of endless brushings he didn't have to pretend to dislike.

Chapter Five

Mikos

MIKOS STARTLED AWAKE, A muffled "the stray!" escaping past his lips.

"Oh, claws and balls" he thought to himself, *"I've napped way too long. Why on earth did I think leaving a newly abandoned stray to Calix's attention was a good idea?"*

He saw a formal reprimand in his future. At least it wasn't dark out yet, he hadn't napped all that long.

Jumping down from his pillow Mikos trotted to the door and started demanding to be let out. He had to get down to the quay fast and find that stray before he or she got up to too much trouble.

His human wasn't responding so he began to pace back and forth, calling out "door, door, dooooor, DOOooorrr, DOOOOOOOORRRR", louder and louder until he was sure he had his human's attention.

The squeak of a chair emanated from the other room as his human called out, making noises at him. She shuffled up to the door and opened it up a crack. Mikos was out in a flash, sprinting down some steps to the quay, hoping he wasn't too late to meet with the stray and establish some authority.

In minutes he was crossing the seaside road and leaping up to that flat surface along the shore. He scanned both directions, fearing that the stray had already gone, or been taken somewhere by Calix and Nyke.

Apparently though, not much had happened. He caught sight of the three of them, silhouetted in the evening light, moving toward one of Calix's favorite scavenging spots.

Mikos headed after them, a little surprised they were still here. It looked as if the stray had only just moved from the spot, he had seen her sitting earlier in the day. Had she really sat there all day unmoving?

"That's something to really make your whiskers droop" he thought.

She, he could see her more clearly now and smell the scent of her on the wind, definitely a she, and pregnant to boot. She must have sat there waiting for her humans to come back, unwilling to fathom that they'd left her behind on purpose.

Mikos heaved a sad sigh to himself. It was always harder for those types to acclimatize themselves to life in Poros. There was the council and their rules, and even though the humans put out food regularly and sometimes the fishing humans would toss them a fresh catch, life was far from easy here. Unless you had human caretakers, like Mikos did, and there were few willing caretakers on Poros. Those abandoned cats who had been previously well cared for and pampered always had a hard time accepting this change in their lives.

While contemplating all of this, Mikos caught up to them, he had heard the constant drone of Calix's voice as he approached, but there was silence now.

The stray had frozen for some reason. He didn't know what to do.

"Should I interrupt?" he thought, *"say something? Ask Calix or Nyke what is going on?"*

He was uncertain what to do at this point.

"SCRATCHING KITTENS!"

The exclamation and following scream of frustration brought him out of his reverie. *"Well at least that's confirmed,"* he thought. *"Time to introduce myself, I guess."*

Mikos wasn't always that great at reading situations.

He reminded himself of this as she rebuffed him. Then she turned and walked away, leaving him, Nyke and Calix staring after her in silence.

Calix recovered first, her tail flashing in amusement.

"Well Mikos, you've done it now. Looks like she's going to have to learn the hard way. I thought you'd be here sooner. By the way, her name is Dahlia"

"Y-y-yeah, what t-t-took you so long?" asked Nyke.

Mikos lowered his chin, pushing his ears forward at them.

"I was on council business," he said, "which is to say, none of yours"

Calix laughed in his face, her tail flipping back and forth in amusement.

With a snort she said, "Council handing out a good brushing and some food again were they?"

Then she winked at him.

"Some nerve," he thought, but said nothing.

A commotion from the direction of the stray drew his attention. He turned his head just in time to see the kick that sent her skidding across the quay and into the sea.

"Oh, scratch scratch Scratch!" Calix yelled.

She sprinted toward where Dahlia had gone over the edge, Nyke only a moment behind her.

Mikos had barely gotten out a "wha...?" when Calix reached the spot where Dahlia had gone over and then she herself disappeared over the side of the quay. Nyke pulled up short and sat down. Mikos could make out his head turning this way and that as he searched for something down in the water.

Then he turned away from the water, threw his head back, and yowled. He yowled so loudly that a group of gulls took flight to get away from the noise.

Mikos was stunned.

"Is Calix gone? Just like that?" he thought.

Emotions welled up, overwhelming him, and he lifted his voice in symphony with Nyke. He sang his sorrow up toward the sky.

"OH, shut up!" Calix's voice reached out from over the edge. "Stop whining and go pester one of the kinder humans to come pull us out of the water."

And then a much quieter "Males are the worst, amiright?"

Chapter Six

Mikos

UPON HEARING CALIX WHISPERING one of her favorite phrases Mikos let out a huff and strode over to the edge of the quay. Stretching his neck out, he peeked over the side.

Calix and Dahlia were there, clinging to the rough stone side of the quay with their front claws.

Calix was looking up at him.

"Forgot I could swim, did ya?" she said.

"Yes."

"Turns out Dahlia here, also knows."

"I noticed."

Mikos backed away at the sound of heavy footsteps.

Nyke, who'd run off, came running back, tail straight up in the air, meowing for all he was worth. Mikos watched as he started circling the spot where the other two had gone over the side. The human that followed kept speaking gently and calmly to him.

"They all LOVE Nyke" Mikos thought, *"I wonder if they can tell he stutters."*

Many cats made a habit of discounting Nyke as a simpleton because of his stuttering, it didn't appear as if the humans noticed the difference in his speech patterns though.

"You're grooming bare skin again Mikos" he thought, shaking his head at himself and returning his attention to the human.

Reaching Nyke, the human looked over the edge, and noticed Calix and Dahlia clinging to the side of the quay.

"Ohhhh," it exclaimed - without a fuss it squatted, reached over, and unceremoniously plucked Calix and then Dahlia from the water. Calix traced a few figure eights under the human's open palm, showing her thanks. Dahlia was more wary, as was the human. He didn't recognize her and with her fur soaked and clinging to her body, her pregnancy was unavoidably obvious.

It reached one of its paws out toward her, but she shrank back and looked away.

"It's ok" Calix said "It's one of the good ones and won't hurt you. It might even feed you."

"Now now Calix" Mikos interrupted, "Don't go giving her ideas, the council has to decide where she'll go before we start having her cozy up to any of the humans. You know that."

Calix looked at him hard, seemed about to challenge him, but then dropped the matter. Her ears and head drooped a little, perhaps with exhaustion. The human patted her a couple more times, and then with a glance at Dahlia, stood up and walked back the way it had come.

"We'll have to find a place for her to hide out until I can meet with the rest of the council," Mikos said.

He was watching the human, worried. That one had a habit of taking things into its own hands. It might come back to take Dahlia in, something that had the potential to upset the balance of things on the island. The council's decisions could seem harsh he knew, but they kept them all alive and fed. Before the council had been organized it had been every cat for themselves and any not adopted by a human was likely to succumb to mange, disease, starvation, or worse. It had not been a good time for the cats of Poros—constant fights and quite a bit of suffering.

Still, the council's will wasn't absolute, humans could and often did do things on their own. The council adapted to things as best they could. An abandoned cat on the verge of birthing kittens could attract the attention of any number of humans. If the council acted quickly enough, they could perhaps parade Dahlia in front of a human they chose rather than waiting for one to choose her. It would ease the shuffling everyone would have to do to accommodate the newcomer.

"I kn-kn-know of a pl-place she can hide."

"Hmm?" he looked up at Nyke, "oh yes, um, are you ok handling that on your own Nyke?'

"Of c-c-course.'

"Very well, thank you. Calix, would you be willing to help me track down Hera and Phira?"

"Sure, why not," Calix said.

"My thanks."

Calix flicked her tail at him and scampered off. He turned to Dahlia.

"Please follow Nyke here and hide out until the council can arrange things."

"I would like to speak to this council myself." Dahlia said to him.

He blinked at her. She managed to give off an air of confidence even while soaking wet and looking for all the world like an overstuffed bat.

"I'm sorry," Mikos said, "That's not really how we do things, what happens is..."

"I don't care!" she shouted, striding up to him and batting him on the face with her paw.

"I'm exhausted, I'm hungry, I'm pregnant, and, for the last time, I. Am. Royalty. You all had better start treating me as such. Where is your shrine to Bastet?"

"Who?"

Dahlia looked askance at him, she seemed genuinely shocked at the question.

"P-p-please Dahlia, the p-p-place I know of is c-c-comfortable and I will bring you s-s-something to eat."

After a moment, Dahlia seemed to warm to Nyke's offer.

"Fine," she said, "but Mikos. I still want to meet with this council."

Mikos tried to stare her down, but her hard eyes didn't even give the impression they could flinch, and he looked away.

"I will see what I can do." he said, turning and trotting away to look for the other counselors.

"Who the scratch is Bastet?" he thought to himself as he ran into an alley and dashed up the stairs.

Chapter Seven

Dahlia

DAHLIA WATCHED MIKOS AS he made his way from the quay, crossing the seaside road and disappearing into shadows made by the buildings and shops fronting the town of Poros.

She thought him a handsome and regal looking male. His long fur was attractive, especially with those glorious stripes. She could see how he had ended up on whatever this "council" was. He gave every impression of being a leader. She briefly considered him as a mate, a king to rule by her side. Then a question popped into her mind.

"How can so many cats not know of Bastet?"

When she was younger, she had been taught that Bastet looked over all cats everywhere and held dominion over them. She had a difficult time understanding why she kept running into those who'd never heard of her before.

Movement from inside her belly brought her back to reality. She sighed.

"No sense in thinking of taking any thrones in my condition." she thought to herself, *"Who knows the lineage of these little ones? What a mess this is."*

She looked at Nyke and was startled when she found him contemplating her intently, way more intelligence reflected in his eyes than she thought possible for him. He noticed her noticing and seemed to consider that too, then he looked to the town.

"W-w-we should go" he said.

Calix's quip about males being the worst suddenly came back to her.

"I thought Calix was male." she blurted out loud, "She carries the scent of one."

"I assure you sh-sh-she is inexorably f-f-female, but that is Calix's s-s-story, if she wishes to tell it"

A hint of claw and challenge had entered Nyke's voice, she noticed. She decided on a different topic.

"Fair enough. Do you, at least, know of Bastet?"

"I have n-n-never heard that n-n-name before." He said, "Now p-p-please, if you would, f-f-follow me"

"I'll stay right where I am, thank you." she replied.

She had some questions, and Nyke, gentle as he was, seemed the most likely to give her straight answers. Looking at him though, Dahlia realized she may have underestimated him. Some of her arrogance melted away.

"I mean, I'll go with you, but could you answer some questions first?"

"Very well"

He sat down and looked at her, waiting patiently.

"Smart play that," Dahlia thought to herself, then to Nyke.

"What is this place?"

"P-p-poros, an island in a human land called G-g-greece.

"Never heard of it," she said, mostly to herself.

"Well, f-f-fortunately for me, it exists d-d-despite you not kn-kn-knowing of it."

Dahlia's head cocked at the joke. Nyke was looking right at her, amusement obvious by his posture. Dahlia drew herself up, matching him stare for stare.

"I'll thank you for not playing coy with me! I have not in any way been false with you, mock me at your peril!"

Nyke had the grace to look embarrassed and looked away.

"You are right, I apologize for teasing you," he said.

Then he looked back to her, his ears moving in a query."

"Are you not h-h-hungry?"

She could not tell if she was hungry or not. She thought she was, or at least thought she should be.

"Odd, how long has it been since I ate?" She thought to herself.

To Nyke though, she said. "Some things are more important than hunger."

"S-s-suit yourself."

They both quieted. The sounds of life on the quay filtered through the air around them.

Some big human ship passing through let out a long low whistle. Nyke glanced at it, then back at her. He seemed nervous about it, on edge.

Dahlia sighed, "What?"

Nyke looked back at the ship, gestured to it with his nose.

"In a little b-b-bit, that boat is going to d-d-drop off a bunch of humans. They will f-f-fill up the quay, making it m-m-more dangerous for us. Please, if you would, f-f-follow me. I know s-s-somewhere safer we can s-s-speak."

"In a moment," she said.

For the first time since she had been abandoned here, Dahlia was taking this place in. The long quay stretched out before her in either direction. Boats of all different sizes and colors lined it. Some floating a little way out, others secured to the quay in a manner that allowed them to rise and fall with the tide.

On the quay itself, periodic piles of nets glistened in the sun, a testament to the fishing humans who made a living here. Also, along the quay, were human tables, neatly covered with cloth and adorned with all sorts of human objects. Huge umbrellas rose up on poles, their domed tops open, creating shade and providing relief from the heat of the sun. She assumed differing patterns denoted different eating establishments among humans.

Other cats roamed among these tables, occasionally approaching humans that looked to be eating. She noticed some were friendly with humans while others remained more skittish, pretending to be afraid but willing, if the right kind of food were offered, to interact. Here and there some cats lounged around doing nothing at all, content to lay in the sun and soak up the warmth.

What Dahlia didn't see were any starving and mangy cats. Cats who were ill or had trouble moving about seemed absent also. She saw one, with long dark fur, that appeared to have a broken front leg, but that was it.

She remembered her mother admonishing her to stay away from those whose fur was thin, their skin covered in sores, lest she catch the malady herself and become unapproachable by the humans.

"Where were they all?" she wondered to herself.

She looked back to Nyke, only to find him watching the ship, a nervous edge in his stance that hadn't been there before.

"Perhaps he doesn't like crowds?" she wondered. She decided to ease his nervousness and get on with things.

"Very well, I am ready to follow you" she said to him.

He jumped at the sound of her voice, his eyes darting back to look at her. Then he calmed.

"Th-th-this way." he said and led her off the quay, across the street and up into Poros proper.

No sooner had they gotten past the first row of buildings when a familiar voice pulled them up short.

"Sheesh, took you long enough, I'll take it from here Nyke."

Calix was resting at the top of some stairs, one terrace up, looking down at them. Nyke blinked an acknowledgement then veered off and disappeared without a word, leaving Dahlia standing there alone looking up at Calix. A position she did not at all like. Calix's eyes followed Nyke as he left them, then she turned a hard gaze upon Dahlia.

"We need to talk," was all she said as she turned and ran up another flight of steps.

"Smart" she thought, *"If I want answers, I've no choice but to follow."*

And that's what she did, her curiosity getting the better of her.

Chapter Eight

Dahlia

DAHLIA RAN AFTER CALIX as she dashed up three flights of steps in quick succession, barely pausing as she moved from one to the next. At the top of the third flight, they came to a narrow road. Calix turned left, crossed the road, and then scampered on, hugging the edge of a low terrace wall.

Dahlia followed suit, but she was getting tired, she couldn't remember ever having to move her body up so many steps. The ship she'd lived on had one short flight of steps, more of a leaping affair than climbing. This was climbing, and Dahlia was beginning to feel it as her breathing became more and more labored.

Calix stopped right before a bend in the road and sniffed the air, then the wall right next to her.

Turning to Dahlia she said, "Wait here a second will you?"

Before Dahlia could reply she turned and disappeared around the bend. A few seconds later, Dahlia heard the hissing of an argument echo from the other side of the wall she was standing against.

"Come on Fluff, clear out. I need this space for a bit." she heard Calix say with authority.

Another voice answered, apparently "Fluff"

"Oh come on Cal, you know this is my favorite napping spot. Why do you have to hang out in my territory anyway?"

"I need the space Fluff, got a newly abandoned with me, want to talk to her."

"Well, I'm not stopping you."

"Privately."

A sharp edge had entered Calix's voice. Dahlia found her own claws extending in response to the tone. She didn't want to think about what the other cat was going through, confronted by all of Calix rather than just her voice.

Calix is a power here, Dahlia realized, even if she isn't on the council everyone keeps mentioning. Another thing tugged at Dahlia's memory, something she was curious about. Oh yes! If Calix was a female, why did she smell like a male? Dahlia was very confused by this, having never encountered it before. She didn't question it, everyone so far had treated Calix as a female, and Dahlia would as well. She just wanted to understand.

"Although" she thought to herself, *"I'm about to have who knows how many little ones demanding my attention. I should probably stop wondering why everyone calls Calix a she when she smells like a he."*

"Priorities Dahlia, " she mumbled out loud.

Just then, the argument Calix and Fluff had been having, the one she'd stopped paying attention to, apparently reached its climax.

There was some rustling and yowling, the sounds of a short fight and then a dark colored male flashed from around the bend and sprinted past her down the road. She watched as he ran away and saw him stop at a rise. He turned to look at her, as if wanting to get a peek at the cause of his nap's disruption. With his eyes wide open and his head raised a little, he looked as if he was half expecting her or Calix to come chasing after him. Seeing that no one was following, his manner relaxed a little.

"You owe me Calix!" he said with the loud uncertainty of someone embarrassed by betters.

"Sure thing Fluff" Calix's voice responded from right beside Dahlia, causing her to jump straight up in the air as if a spring and gone off underneath her.

"OH BASTET!" she squealed in mid-air.

She landed facing Calix, spoiling for a fight.

She lowered her ears and dropped her head, getting ready to make a move toward Calix's throat.

"Why would you startle me like that?! Just picking on the new cat for your own amusement? Scratch Bastet and scratch you! I've had it with you, with this place! Everyone is so... Weird! So Wrong! None of you knows anything of the world and not a single one of you has treated me with the respect I deserve!"

Calix hadn't moved. She sat there looking down at Dahlia, face completely passive, giving no indication as to what her next move might be, or how she would respond. Dahlia's tail whipped back and forth as she continued her tirade, yelling up at Calix through clenched teeth.

Fluff was long gone, wanting no part of this.

"I'm soaked! I just found out I'm having kittens! Your scratching humans kicked me into the water and there's cats sitting on councils that apparently dictate where we can and can't go to demand food. On top of all of that I was... I wa... I... I...."

It was all too much. With a hiss of frustration Dahlia launched herself at Calix.

Instead of meeting her attack Calix whirled about and disappeared around the bend in the road, Dahlia at her heels. The road curved through the bend, but the wall ended. Calix did a quick U-turn into a triangular nook separate from the road. An old workbench lined one wall, stuff piled up on it, forming a V shaped cranny, Fluff's napping spot.

Dahlia barely noticed, she was out for blood and Calix had finally turned to face her, she was ready, or at least thought she was.

In her hazy rage-fueled vision she didn't really see what Calix did or how she did it, but before she could so much as bite or scratch at Calix, Dahlia found herself pinned to the ground, wrapped in Calix's forelegs.

She squirmed, trying to get herself rolled over so she could bring her hind feet into play, to push Calix off or rake her with her claws. Then she felt it, the rough sandpaper feel of Calix's tongue lapping at her forehead, cleaning and grooming her. The act enraged her all the more and Dahlia struggled harder to free herself from Calix's grip, to turn this into a proper fight.

Spitting and hissing, she railed at Calix. An unintelligible stream of profanity, throwing every hurtful word she'd ever learned at Calix.

Calix kept right on grooming her.

Dahlia's tirade ended with a shout "You let me go Calix... I... I!"

"You were abandoned" Calix said calmly, gently, stopping her grooming long enough to whisper the words.

"The humans who cared for you, comforted you, fed you, kept you safe. Loved you." Calix choked on those last two words, but then finally resumed.

"They. Abandoned. You."

Dahlia completely deflated. To hear it said so openly, the truth she'd been resisting, the reality she'd pushed away by focusing on hunger or anything else fell upon her soul like a heavy rain in turbulent seas.

She lay there, letting the sorrow of loss overtake her as Calix continued her gentle ministrations.

(lick)

OH, how she hated them! At the same time, she missed them so much. Her warring against her desire to climb into a friendly lap once more.

(lick)

"How could they?!"

(lick)

Sobs wracked her body as Calix continued grooming her quietly, gently. Eventually Dahlia's head cleared enough for her to indicate Calix could stop. Calix backed off a little and sat, looking at Dahlia, compassion still evident in her eyes and demeanor.

"Thank you" Dahlia said to her. Finding it difficult to meet Calix's gaze.

Calix blinked an acknowledgement.

"Before anything else could happen, you had to face that. I'm speaking from experience mind you. Scratch it if it doesn't still hurt like hell from time to time."

Dahlia looked around, taking in the surroundings for the first time really. Her eyes narrowed at the day's brightness.

"Besides, you're going to need to be levelheaded when we go to face the Council." Calix said.

"We?"

"Oh, Scratch it all! I jumped into the water to save your life. You think I'm gonna let you face the Council alone without any prep?"

"Well..."

"I know I know; you had other things to deal with. Now that we've cleared your whiskers a little, let's have that talk. There are some other things it's like to talk to you about. Your presence and condition have presented us with a unique opportunity. Are you willing to listen?"

Chapter Nine

Calix

CALIX WATCHED AS A much less tightly wound Dahlia blinked an affirmative to her.

"Ok" Dahlia said "Let's talk. Why do you smell like a male?"

Calix's tail flicked and she looked away.

Turning back to Dahlia she flashed a sardonic grin and said, "The thing is, there's a perfectly good explanation for that."

"And what is that?"

"I'm a female that smells like a male."

Perhaps Dahlia caught the edge of weary resignation in her voice. The exhaustion that can only come from the tedium of having to answer the same question every time some new cat shows up in her life.

"I'm sorry Calix ' she said, "I only ask because one of the places near where I'm from could only have a female ruler by traditional decree. Only they'd outgrown that part, but for some reason they got around it by declaring any ruler they chose to be female. Regardless of if they were male or female. Considering the influence, you've shown yourself to have over this place since we've met, I was wondering if this was a similar type of situation. I didn't mean to question if you were really female or not. I'm only trying to make sense of this place. In the city I am from, females typically rule, specifically those coated like the night but bearing the mark of Bastet. I, I don't know, your scent confused me..."

The words had come out of Dahlia in a rush. She looked out of breath and a little embarrassed at having to explain herself so.

Taken from her home at a young age, trying to maintain some semblance of home in her environment, alone among the humans. Shockingly naive and ignorant about some things, yet well-traveled and cosmopolitan in others. The things Dahlia must have seen as her humans sailed her from place to place. Calix had never heard of Bastet, or even of any cats having a goddess to worship at all.

"Goddesses are a thing of humans, not us" she thought to herself.

Still, she found herself experiencing some wanderlust, a longing to see the parts of the world Dahlia must have seen and experienced.

"Where are you from?" she asked Dahlia.

Dahlia looked off, eyes going distant as if chasing a memory forever out of reach.

"I don't remember its name."

She lay down and rested her head on her paws for a moment, then raised it to look Calix in the eyes.

"I think the place is called Egypt, or Agypt, but I'm not sure. All I have to go on is a bunch of cats from another land telling me of Bastet that, "gods from Egypt mean nothing to us". As for where in Egypt? I don't know. I was very young and hadn't ventured out so much. The very first group of humans I approached for food snatched me up and took me with them. That was that, until..."

She trailed off and rested her head on her paws again.

"How long ago?" Calix asked.

"I don't know Calix. I was so young, and time isn't easy to keep track of when you're moving from place to place. Long enough for me to grow up and get pregnant though" she said bitterly.

"And you stopped at many places?"

Dahlia huffed.

"I tire of this Calix, aren't we supposed to talk about meeting the council?"

"So, some bitterness there," Calix thought. *"I'll ask her about it another time."*

"I have one more question for you." Calix ventured, "You say you're royalty? Are you a queen where you come from?"

Dahlia's ears perked up a little at this question. She was definitely more open to discussing this part of her life.

"I was supposed to be. My mother was, at least she was around the group of human buildings where we lived. The wealthiest family of humans cared for her, and she had complete authority over the other cats in her domain. I was to replace her someday. I was the only child she'd born that also bore the mark of Bastet.

She said she'd given birth to two other litters before I was born and told me she'd prayed at our shrine to Bastet every day for a successor. Said I was a blessing from the goddess herself. That this mark on my chest meant it was my destiny to take her throne when she moved on to the goddess's domain."

"But then the humans took you?" Calix asked, utterly fascinated.

"Bastet blessed me with my own humans, yes. For a while at least. I don't know what happened to my mother, or siblings. I hope she was able to birth another successor."

Calix had no more questions and Dahlia seemed content to sit in silence.

Still Calix's mind raced, active as ever. She understood Dahlia now. At least a little bit. Understood how she could be so knowledgeable about some things and ignorant of others. She could see it in her mind's eye. The humans moving from place to place, young Dahlia in tow, brain filled with incomplete knowledge of the world. She'd talk to and learn from other cats on quays and docks all over the place. Picking up bits of pieces of knowledge and minutiae specific to dozens of different towns and ports. Small wonder she could speak well but had had no idea she was pregnant. Detailed knowledge of mating, giving birth, and raising kittens would have been denied her in the everyday banter between the ship born nomads and those that lived on land.

Calix wished she could track down the male who'd taken advantage of Dahlia's ignorance and mated her on that boat.

"Track him down and chew if balls off,"

He'd have been aware that she wouldn't know the routines, wouldn't know how to decline his advance.

"Males are the scratching worst." Calix mumbled aloud.

"Mmm?"

"Oh nothing, don't worry about it."

Calix drifted back to her own thoughts once more, trying to imagine all the possible places Dahlia must have visited. She looked down and opened her mouth to speak. Dahlia was fast asleep, curled up upon herself, snoring softly. Calix leaned down and gently licked the top of Dahlia's head a couple of times. Then a rustle from below drew her attention and she looked down over the edge of the workbench. Fluff was back, no doubt wanting his spot back.

"Might need your spot a little longer Fluff." she said.

"I can hear, but Cal, there's a storm coming. Can't you smell it?"

Calix sniffed the air. There was indeed a storm coming.

"Won't be here until tonight, by the smell of it." she said.

"Also," Fluff continued, "Mikos is looking for you, nobody can locate Phira it seems. Oh, and Nyke said to tell you he's ready."

"Ah,ok. Thanks Fluff, I owe you some souvlaki."

"You bet your tail you do. I won't be forgetting either."

Fluff turned and ran out of the nook to wherever he waited out storms. Nyke appeared at the nook's entrance and sat down, waiting. Calix chirped at him and his tail flicked in amusement, then she turned and nudged Dahlia until she woke up, her green eyes swiveling up to focus on her.

"We should move. Nyke is here, he knows somewhere safe and has it ready for you. He'll stay with you if you want or need him to. There's also the other matter I mentioned"

Dahlia's ears twitched in agreement.

"You also might want to prepare yourself for the possibility that certain things may come to a head before you can meet the council."

Dahlia put up no resistance. She yawned, stretched her body out, over-balanced and fell right out of the sleeping nook, bounced off the side of the work bench and landed on all fours right in front of Nyke. The expression on her face said she had no idea what just happened to her.

Calix almost fell off herself, she was laughing so hard.

Dahlia turned to look up at her.

"Funny" she said dryly, and followed Nyke, who'd already started away.

Calix half watched them go, lost in thought, lost in old memories.

Fear

A car ride,

Strange human gripping her tightly,

The door opening and then a sense of flying.

The feel of weeds and thorns scraping against her body as she was flung into the brush.

Rolling roughly across the ground to the sound of squealing tires and a fading engine roar.

Thunder rumbling off in the distance brought her back to the present.

Calix hadn't quite been abandoned. Her human had died when she was young, and the ones who'd come after had dropped her out in the wilderness. It was a small miracle she'd made it to Poros. She'd had to fight with the council for decent treatment, but she'd won a place for herself, all while suffering the pain of losing her human.

She'd vowed to always help newly abandoned or newly homeless strays any time she came across them. Even if it meant challenging the council's edicts. They were fair in their own way, but too tied to tradition and often unable to adapt. So, Calix played the counterweight to their unbalanced view. They somewhat respected her. Mostly because she'd trounced each member in a fight at one time or another, but hey that's how it was with cats.

Her mind turned back to the business at hand, Calix leapt off the workbench and trotted off to go find Mikos.

A very faint flicker of lightning flashed in the distance.

Chapter Ten

Calix

THE BUSTLE OF LIFE echoed around Poros as Calix roamed the terraces, searching for Mikos. Behind her a wake of greetings and regards spread outward as if she were some small fishing boat cruising along the calm waters of the bay.

"Hey Cal."

"Where ya going Calix?"

"Calix! Did you remember to..."

"Cal, dammit you owe me a..."

She didn't stop, barely even heard. Her ears and tail acted out a greeting when necessary, she ignored the rest.

"Break it to her gently Nyke." she whispered to herself as if her words could weave a spell that would find its way to Nyke, willing things to go as she hoped.

"Whatever you do, don't let her wander off on her own." She'd said to him.

He'd acknowledged the instruction quietly, as was his way.

She took a deep breath to calm her worries, she trusted Nyke. Completely. She would be better off remembering that.

"Hey Calix, Mikos is looking for you, just saw him..."

Calix pulled up short, looking toward the source of that voice.

"Where?" she asked.

"One up, over by Saffron's" came the reply.

"Thanks" Calix finished, moving on up the lane.

She picked up her pace and climbed up to the next terrace. Not bothering with the human made roads and stairs, she chose to make a straight line for Saffron's, weaving through the brush, and scaling the rocky rises. This high up, there was plenty of open land to climb on.

"Mikos!" she began shouting as she neared Saffron's

"MIKOS! Where are you, scratch it!? MIIIKKKOOOSSSSSSSSSSS!"

That last came out in a long loud yowl. Loud enough to attract the attention of a human, who threw something at her.

Calix watched as, whatever it was, sailed through the air, landing some ways aways from her. Then Miko's voice sounded from higher up.

"I'm here, I'm here, up by the tower, no need to shout so loudly."

Turning and trotting up toward the tower she shouted up to him.

"What are you doing up here, you big oaf?"

"Nobody knows where Phira is, I thought she might be up here. You know she likes to come here sometimes, just to be away from everything"

"Mikos." Calix said calmly.

"We must find her Calix. We've got to get the council together so a decision can be reached before..."

"Mikos." Calix repeated, a little more sternly

"But nobody's seen her Calix, nobody seems to know where she..."

Calix snapped.

"Stop turning your belly up Mikos! You know scratch well this isn't going to wait for the council!"

He looked at her aghast and slightly confused.

"Wha..." He managed to get out before she continued.

"Listen, you saw what I saw. You would have to be an absolute moron with your tail stuffed into your brain not to have noticed. Dahlia, that pregnant cat abandoned on the quay earlier today, is going to have her kittens..."

"Surely there's..."

"She's going to give birth Mikos, TONIGHT. You know it's going to be tonight, don't fuck around with me on this."

Mikos relaxed as if finally accepting something he hadn't wanted to be true.

"Yes, yes, you're correct. The kittens will come tonight. It was obvious. I thought if we could get the council together in time and decide which human to present her to, we could have at least gotten her into a safe space to give birth..."

He trailed off for a minute...

Then more quietly.

"... but I can't find Phira"

Calix laughed half in amusement, her tail flashing back at fourth impatiently as she contemplated the best way to bring Mikos the rest of the way to reality.

Finally, she spoke.

"Mikos, you're too kind by half and too trusting by a third. You know scratch well Hera wouldn't have let anything be decided tonight. Even with Phira on your side, she'd have advised waiting and the others would have backed her"

"Honestly, I thought your involvement would tip the balance".

Calix flopped down on the ground and laughed.

"How!?" she managed to get out, "You know Hera hates me."

She rolled around in amusement, playfully teasing Mikos, easing his tension.

"I thought she might jump in to help instead, just to spite you."

Calix stopped rolling.

"Huh" she thought to herself, *"that might have actually worked. Probably not though."*

To Mikos she said.

"Wow Mikos, I didn't think you had it in you. Kindness, yes. Compassion, yes, Honor, yes. Manipulative Cleverness, nope. Perhaps I'm rubbing off on you."

Mikos looked at her, lying there rolling on the ground, and snorted.

"Yikes, humans snatch me if that's the case."

His joking manner indicated he was ready to hear what Calix had to say next.

"We have to help her Mikos. Without the council's approval. There's no time to get the humans involved anyway. I've got her set up at our resting place with Nyke. It's as prepared as it can be. She should be able to give birth there with no trouble. There's a storm coming so maybe that will keep them from finding her and the kittens but..."

"Yes, but..." Mikos replied, "Elmax and Ajax"

Calix involuntarily shuddered.

There weren't any stray dogs in Poros, she had no idea why, but some humans kept and took care of some dogs in the same manner many did with cats. For the most part the cats and the Council got along with them. There were a couple treaties and informal understandings. Some were actually friends.

Elmax and Ajax were a different story. Their human was a mean ass tom of a human and they reflected that personality perfectly. They were kept behind a fence, and for the most part stayed behind it. Sometimes though, they would get out at night and prowl the terraces of Poros. Any cat, or any animal really, unlucky enough to get cornered by them, ended up dead. The less said of how, the better.

The Council had set up a watch and warning system for them, where watchers would stay out of reach but follow them around meowing out a warning of their passing. Different cats watched different sections of the town, making sure no single cat had to follow them around the whole night, or however long they prowled. It was a good system, but a mother with a newly birthed litter of kittens was especially vulnerable, and while Elmax and Ajax didn't terrorize the steps and alleys of Poros every night, if one of them caught a whiff of newborn kittens, they would come. The approaching storm could be a blessing or a curse. On one hand, it could mask the scent of a cat giving birth. On the other side though, the watchers would be unable to follow and give warning. If Elmax and Ajax came, they wouldn't know about it until they were there, snarling and snapping in their faces.

"We may have to fight them," Calix said somberly.

"We may have to fight who?" a new voice said imperiously.

"Ugh, of course SHE would show up," Calix thought to herself in annoyance.

Turning, she forced her ears into as passive a position as she could muster.

"Good evening, Hera," she said as sweetly and nasally as she could, "how are things?"

Chapter Eleven

Dahlia

NYKE WOVE THEM A path through Poros. Dahlia kept her attention on his tail and followed, lost in her own thoughts. She was aware that Nyke had to keep pausing to make sure she was following, and that he was a little annoyed by this.

She didn't care, too much had happened in one day for her to care all that much about anything really. Abandoned, pregnant, dumped in the water, having to meet (and trust) new cats. Dahlia was in full situational overload, her body desperately wanting to shut down, her mind, exhausted but racing all the same.

Dahlia stumbled as they scampered up a stairwell.

Nyke turned, came back down to her and whispered,

"W-we are almost there, n-n-not much farther."

Dahlia blinked an acknowledgement and he continued.

Marshaling her strength, she followed after him, up stony steps, along a smooth wooden porch railing, across the tiled roof of some shed and then to a wall that lined the edge of the terrace shielding a narrow lane.

They moved along the top of this wall for a bit until Nyke abruptly jumped down, crossed the small lane, and disappeared into a hole in a thick bush growing in a lee of one of the human houses.

Dahlia followed and was surprised to see a small tunnel through the brush that ended in a semicircular cavern nestled under the thick branches of the bush and enclosed on two sides by the walls of the human home. Nyke sat there looking at her, dry leaves rustled as the tip of his tail whipped back and forth pensively.

"Pl-please wait h-h-here a moment, I will be r-r-right back. I p-p-promise" he said.

Dahlia looked around. The place seemed comfortable enough, warm and dry. A pretty good spot to weather the night actually. Dahlia swiveled her ears and averted her eyes.

"I will wait." she said.

Nyke dipped his head in reply and exited back through the tunnel without a word. Dahlia began exploring the space, searching for the most comfortable spot to lay down and curl up. She noticed a spot that was fairly well coated with Nyke's and Calix's fur, their scents unmistakable. She moved to that spot, tested out the soft cover of leaves with her paws. Her eyes closed as she purred, the contentment of feeling her claws extend and retract, extend and retract, relaxed muscles she hadn't realized were knotted. Sighing inwardly, she poured body into the spot, the gathering of leaves already working to gather her body's warmth and give it back. Resting her chin on her paws, Dahlia let out a long slow breath. Her ears twitched a little toward the sound of rustling branches, Nyke returning. She chose to ignore it. She felt him approach her and then something thumped onto the ground right in front of her face. She opened her eyes to see what it was, but her nose beat them to recognition. Saliva flooded her mouth as the smell of fresh fish flooded her nostrils.

One of her paws flashed out and she stomped, sinking her claws into it while growling and staring down Nyke, who backed off a little. Keeping an eye on him, she began to eat. So entranced she was by feeding, she was unaware Nyke had left and come back with another fish until he plopped it down in front of her.

She ate that one too.

As her need to eat subsided and some semblance of civility entered her mind again, she looked to Nyke.

"Thank you, I don't know that I'd have done the same for you"

"P-p-perhaps we shall find out one d-d-day. Besides, you n-n-need your wits about you f-f-for what I have to tell you."

"And what is that?"

"S-s-something for a little later, I think. D-d-do you have any more q-q-questions for me? I think it's s-s-safe to say you've earned a few answers."

He regarded her quietly as she thought about this.

"What do I want to know?" she wondered.

She looked at Nyke, the black and gray stripes of his hood, his white snout, chest and legs. He seemed a bit on the small side, and she could imagine many treating him as if he were stupid because of his stutter, but Dahlia had met too many different cats from different places to fall into that bias. A fierce intelligence sparkled in his eyes despite his calm demeanor. An intelligence apparent in everything he chose to say and do, if one bothered to listen.

"Hmmm Let's surprise him and see how he reacts."

She opened her mouth and asked, "Why do you let Calix boss you around?"

"What m-m-makes you think I do?"

"You respond with questions after saying I've earned answers?"

"Calix d-d-does not b-b-boss me around."

Dahlia was a little taken aback by this. She wasn't expecting so forward an answer.

"I clearly saw her ordering you around and teasing you for that matter. Also, in front of both me and that other cat Mikos, she treated you as if you were rather dense. In bringing me to this place and feeding me you were clearly following her instructions and you appear to be fiercely loyal to her. What I'd like to know is why, because I can clearly see that you are much more intelligent than she was giving you credit for. Why would you put up with that?"

Nyke looked at her with no apparent reaction. Then she noticed the tip of his tail twitching back and forth and she realized he was amused. She looked back at his face and watched his eyes close in silent laughter. Before she could say anything more though, he replied.

"It w-w-was my idea to s-s-set up our apparent dynamic like that. C-c-calix the loud one everyone looks t-t-to, me the one who g-g-gets the little things done."

"So, who's in charge?" Dahlia asked.

"We are." came the simple reply.

This was a novel idea for Dahlia. Being born into a monarchy and not coming across many variations on this in her travels, the thought of two cats working together as equals was very strange to her. She saw the power in it though, the face they put on for others. She'd seen how it was with Mikos. Calix's brazen and boisterous attitude drew all the attention and deferment, but also her casually harsh treatment of Nyke had seemed to make Mikos more respectful and considerate of him. It was as if Calix's treatment offended the other cats to the point where they treated Nyke as the kind, incredibly intelligent cat he actually was without a second thought.

Dahlia was nodding to herself when Nyke's voice interrupted her thoughts.

"Calix hates that p-p-part. She loves being c-c-crass and glib with the others but treating me like a f-f-fool lackey just so THEY won't has never sat well in her b-b-belly."

"How could you know what I was thi...."

"It was obvious."

"So you're a team? Why? To what end?"

"To be able t-t-to act in certain situations when waiting for the c-c-council would take too long. There are a f-f-few others allied w-w-with us. F-f-fluff, who believe you've m-m-met, and a c-c-couple of others. Most t-t-turn a tail t-t-o our activities but will not ch-chal-lenge the council directly. A c-c-couple council members are fr-friendly to us. Mikos and another named S-s-sable."

"What type of situations do you involve yourselves in?"

"Like the s-s-situation we f-f-find ourselves in right now."

"And what "situation" is that?" Dahlia huffed, a little put out at being referred to in that manner.

Nyke spat as if he was about to strike her but didn't really want to. He seemed to have a brief argument with himself about the time but then squared up to her, looking her right in the eyes. To her, his eyes appeared full of compassion and kindness laced with difficult decisions and hard living. Looking at them Dahlia understood the dedication he brought to anything he cared about and knew that she currently fell into that category.

She was oddly comforted by this. Which was good because what he said next struck her right on the nose with all five claws extended.

"I'm sorry, wha-what did you just say?!" she asked.

"Your k-k-kittens, by all appearances, you will give b-b-birth to them tonight."

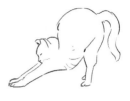

Chapter Twelve

Dahlia

DAHLIA SAT SILENT FOR several moments with Nyke's revelation. She pondered it. Then she scoffed.

"Oh please, no I'm not. I know I wasn't entirely aware of my condition before, but I think I'd notice if my body was about to start expelling kittens. My Lady will guide me when the time comes."

Nyke watched her, his expression unreadable. His tail gave a single swipe of annoyance.

"You p-p-put so much faith in this Lady Bastet. W-w-why?"

Dahlia sighed and adjusted her body, adopting a less formal pose with Nyke. 'These will likely be my companions from now on,' she thought to herself 'might as well learn to be comfortable with them'.

"I was raised to rule a family, my status bestowed by this mark on my chest, the Kiss of Bastet. I had barely learned of this before I was granted human servants of my own and whisked away to a life aboard the craft they used to travel on the great sea.

For a long time, I thought they had been sent to me by my Lady. Sent to carry me away to a place and household of my own. The humans certainly cared for me as if I was their ruler. They fed me, gave me attention whenever

I demanded it, taught me how to swim and ensured I knew how to climb back aboard if I ever fell into the water. They would bring me treats and toys, play with me and snuggle with me on cold nights.

I've seen so many places, every stop somewhere new. Sometimes they would even take me with them when they roamed about at one stop or another."

"You c-c-could keep up with them?" Nyke's ears flicked in doubt.

Dahlia purred in amusement, lost in her memories.

"They had a basket they'd carry me in." she said wistfully "The inside was coated in some soft cloth, and I'd sit in it, forepaws on the rim, watching all the interesting things go by as they carried me about."

She blinked her eyes slowly at the memory.

She missed them, she realized, her humans. *"Scratch them!"*

To Nyke she continued.

"It was in that way and on our frequent stops that I met many others and began to learn all sorts of things about the world. Learned that Bastet was not known everywhere, even thorough I was loathe to accept it. "

How they'd laughed at her, that first group she'd come across that had had no idea who Lady Bastet was. Laughed much like Calix had down on the quay, though truth be told she felt a little embarrassed for rolling out her imperious self in that situation.

She had been scared and when that happened, she usually tried to act like her mother, who'd been so commanding and sure in her power.

"I learned quite a bit, and eventually understood that our world is much larger than I'd ever realized or been able to comprehend. There is so much variety, you've no idea, but also many similarities."

Dahlia drifted off in her thoughts for a moment, then shook her head.

"Anyway, I hold on to my Lady, because she is all I have left of my first life, all I have left of my mother and siblings, my first home. Even with humans to care for me, I was astray and needed something to anchor me, to hold me to me. That is why I hold faith in my Lady Bastet, and will likely pass this faith to my little ones when the time comes"

She looked Nyke dead in the eyes, daring him to say something chiding or challenging.

Instead, his eyes slowly closed, and a deep rumble began to emanate from his chest.

The expression of empathy touched her, and she found herself reaching out, one paw extended to lightly brush against one of his.

He acknowledged this by lowering his body and making himself more comfortable. Assuming a position her humans had called "cat loaf" and found worthy of much attention for some reason.

Dahlia swatted the memories away, lest they overwhelm her.

"Thank you, f-f-for sharing your s-s-story. I understand now."

"Good, you can be the one to explain it to everyone else then."

Nyke rumbled in amusement.

"Would you like t-t-to know anything in r-r-return?"

Dahlia thought for a moment.

"Yes. What is the council and why is the council?"

"A v-v-very long story."

"You have somewhere to be?"

Nyke tensed inexplicably for a moment, then relaxed.

"V-v-very well, I will t-t-tell you what I know."

Dahlia kneaded the ground, settling in to listen.

"I want to s-s-start by saying, most of us are s-s-strays. We've either b-b-been abandoned by humans, lost from them with n-n-no way home, or been b-b-born into this life. Though s-s-some, such as Mikos, live with h-h-humans, most do not."

Dahlia dipped her ears and blinked. "Noted"

"Many generations ago, things were v-v-very different. There was f-f-food to be had from the fisherman, b-b-but not much else. There were f-f-family groups that ruled the quay and kept any c-c-cats not of them away. For most other p-p-places on the island though, you'd b-b-be on your own. For m-m-most, it was a d-d-difficult and short life. Sometimes, for no r-r-reason, the humans go around and r-r-round up as many cats as they could c-c-capture. Those c-c-caught would never b-b-be seen again.

Then, one d-d-day, the humans began leaving out f-f-food for us all over the island. No-one knows why. Some s-s-speculate it is out of c-c-compassion, others believe they d-d-do it to draw part of the population away from the q-q-quay and the human f-f-feeding places. The truth is anyone's guess.

Eventually, g-g-groups formed to control the f-f-food sources and who c-c-could access them. Those groups g-g-grew to incorporate every virtually s-s-stray on the island. Over t-t-time their leaders d-d-decided to join forces to govern the f-f-food resources and other c-c-collective duties. Each g-group chose a r-r-representative and the council was born."

Nyke began licking his paw, digging at something that had gotten wedged underneath a claw.

"Do these groups have names?" Dahlia asked.

"Some, they're mostly used as honorifics at this point." he dropped his paw back to the ground, "Nowadays every c-c-council member is chosen b-b-by an island-wide v-v-vote whenever a s-s-seat becomes vacant."

"What does the council do?"

"F-f-finds a place for new s-s-strays to fit in, plans out r-r-rotations for quay d-d-duty, organizes the threat w-w-watch, attempts to m-m-match pregnant cats with humans who might c-c-care for them while their k-k-kittens grow."

Dahlia's ears perked up and her eyes grew wide she looked directly at Nyke.

"What threats?"

Nyke's ears laid back defensively,

"I w-w-wish you'd have let me explain it in the w-w-way I'd planned..."

"What. Threats?" she repeated.

"... and your k-k-kittens are c-c-coming tonight..."

"I know, I just needed to talk a bit," Dahlia moved closer to Nyke, forcing eye contact,

"What... Threats?" She pulled up every bit of her mother's personality to channel into those words.

Nyke shrank back from her a little.

"The one's Calix is c-c-currently gathering allies to try and deal with, should they c-c-come when you're m-m-most vulnerable"

The behavior she'd seen so far from Calix, Nyke and Mikos began to make more sense to her.

"And they come for weak mothers with newborn kittens?" she asked, already knowing the answer.

Nyke drew himself up as if preparing to stand alone against these threats for her, but the fur at the base of his tail had fluffed out, giving away his fear. He met her direct stare, eye to eye, ear to ear.

"Always"

"Tell me." Dahlia said, hoping she sounded as strong and confident as she remembered her mother being.

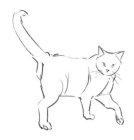

Chapter Thirteen

Calix

"Good evening, Hera," she said as sweetly and nasally as she could, "how are things?"

Calix watched as Hera reacted to her sweetly taunting tone. Ears moving to fold down, a slight arching of her back, lips just starting to curl up in prelude to a hiss. At the last second, she caught herself and maintained her composure.

"They'd be a lot better if you'd tell me what you were up to."

"Oh, you know. Things. Stuff. Other things."

"So, the usual?"

"I am nothing if not consistent."

Calix sat herself up. She needed to get out of this situation before Hera decided to press the issue.

"Well Hera," she said, "I would absolutely LOVE to stay and chat, but I have got some more stuff and things to get up to so..."

"One moment Calix..." Hera interrupted.

"Hmm?"

"Leave the new stray to the council please. We've already gathered, except for Mikos here, and will be discussing what to do very soon. You and Nyke have no need to act on this. If you do attempt anything, I do not know that Sable and Mikos here will be able to save you from the council's reprimand."

"Ahhh, right. Glad that's settled."

Hera looked at her more sternly, bringing her ears forward.

"I mean it Calix, this is what the Council is for, let us deal with it. By the way, where have you got her hidden away?"

Calix returned her gaze, her body expressionless.

"Mikos can tell you." she said, then pretended to cave into uncertainty, "Look I... I really should be going.... Just, just to check on Nyke and the new stray."

Hera, who had been about to interrupt, relented.

"Fine." she said abruptly and turned to Mikos. "Mikos, the council is all gathered and waiting."

"What about Phira?" he said.

"Who do you think called us together?"

Mikos visibly relaxed upon hearing that Phira was present.

"Ok Hera, lead the way"

Calix had been waiting for this moment. She had little improvisation to her and Nyke's plan. A spur of the moment kind of thing she'd thought up when Hera had appeared.

As Mikos and Hera walked away Calix rose and shouted out.

"Hey Mikos!"

They both turned to regard her with wary expressions.

"Don't forget to tell them your idea for dealing with Elmax and Ajax! That was really clever I thought!"

With that, Calix raced off, not giving either a chance to respond. Her tail did give a few amused twitches at the thought of Mikos sputtering while simultaneously trying to tell Hera he had no such ideas. She wouldn't believe him of course. She'd just "caught" him conspiring with Calix.

"Oh Calix" she whispered to herself in satisfaction. "You really are the worst."

Now though, she had to face something far more dangerous. She made her way uphill from the clock tower, eventually coming to the crest of this part of the island. The human dwellings had mostly thinned out at this point save for one. Perched upon a wide flat plot of land at the top of the hill was a single dwelling, the area around it enclosed behind a tall chain link fence.

The home of Elmax and Ajax.

She carefully made her way around the place through the brush, conscious of which direction the wind was blowing from. Taking care not to reveal herself too soon.

She did notice Lucky, today's lookout, sitting in a nearby tree and watching her curiously but ignored him. This part of the plan was delicate and needed to be done without distraction.

She found the spot she needed, in some grass at the base of a large rock almost right up next to the fence, the wind blowing through it and right into the enclosure. She sat herself down on her haunches, facing the fence, and waited. With the wind blowing her scent directly at them, it didn't take long.

A mound of white far behind the fence stirred. Ajax's head lifted, his nose testing the air.

"Calix!" he shouted and in one smooth motion leapt up and began racing straight for her, screaming her name the entire time.

"Calix! Calix! Calix! Calix!"

Calix flinched as he slammed bodily into the fence in front of her. He pushed at it as if he could squeeze himself through one of the tiny holes. Ajax was not all that bright, but what he lacked in intelligence he more than made up for in muscle, exuberance and tenacity. Calix was terrified of Ajax. If he caught you, there was no way out, he would kill you.

Then Elmax was there, shouldering Ajax out of the way to get a look at and sniff at Calix. Elmax was terrifying too, but in a different way. He'd talk to you before he killed you. Calix found that incredibly creepy.

"Calix" Elmax growled out slowly, "have you come to play with us?"

"Play! Play! Play!"

A snap of jaws from Elmax.

"Shut up and let him answer you dimwit!"

"Her," Calix said calmly.

"What? Ajax isn't a her."

"Her. You said, "let HIM answer", I am correcting you. It's Her. We've had this conversation before El."

A growl escaped Elmax's throat.

"I've always been curious as to why you call yourself a female Calix"

"I would imagine confusion was more your style, Elmax"

Calix began casually cleaning one of her paws in front of them. She knew Elmax hated that. He snarled at her, but then quieted.

"We know there's a new stray Calix" he said teasingly, "an expectant mother."

"Stray! Stray! Stray!" echoed Ajax.

"How very observant of you," Calix said between licks "would you also like to comment on the color of the sky?"

"Sky! Sky! Sky!"

"QUIET!" Elmax barked.

Ajax settled a bit, but his back half still shook with barely contained excitement.

"You can't hide her from us Calix, or talk us out of finding her."

Calix examined her claws, extending them out toward her face. She stifled a yawn, feigning boredom.

"I'm not here for that, you imbecile."

"Then what are you doing here?"

She looked at them both, noses pressed to the fence, heads cocked a little to the side.

"Well, here it goes, I hope this works" she thought to herself.

"Claiming what's mine." she said out loud.

As she said this, Calix turned, her tail shot straight up and began to vibrate side to side from the base up. A second later, a stream of urine arched out, soaking the astonished faces of both dogs. She also sprayed the rock for good measure.

Both of them snarled and barked in rage. Pushing up against the fence as if they could crush her with it, but Calix was already gone. Racing away into the grass, out of sight, but not out of mind.

"We'll find you and the stray Calix! We're gonna have so much fun tonight," she heard Elmax howl after her.

Then the barking was silenced by their human, who'd come out to see what the commotion was all about.

Calix, heart pumping as she moved on to her next task muttered.

"Well, that was certainly terrifying."

She paused, taking a few deep breaths to calm herself. After a few moments she turned and looked back toward the way she'd come.

Her eyes gleaming with mischievous satisfaction, she uttered two more words.

"Worth it."

Chapter Fourteen

Mikos

MIKOS SPUTTERED AS CALIX'S parting words echoed through his mind.

"I... I have NO such ideas..."

"Calm down Mikos," Hera assured him, "I'll not say anything. Besides, it's not like anyone would believe You came up with an idea for dealing with those two."

Mikos found himself a touch indignant at Hera's casual dismissal.

"I could have had an idea..."

"Right." Hera replied sardonically.

Mikos quieted. 'It's true,' he thought to himself, 'but why don't I come up with more ideas?'

As they walked on in silence Mikos thought over his life. He was one of the few cats on the island who wasn't a stray. He had specific human caretakers. He had a way into and out of their house, his house. He had many comfy places to sleep and never gone without attention or food.

He knew some of the others resented him for this, but it couldn't be helped. He genuinely cared for his humans, as much as they cared for him.

Still, it was his status as not a stray that had gotten him a seat on the council. They wanted at least one cat that was attached to the humans. One that could advise them on how best to interact with them successfully when something was needed. Although now that he thought about it, the council had never really asked for his assistance in that department either.

"I have become a placeholder for them," he thought, *"someone who votes the way I'm told."*

Realizing this, he became a little disappointed in himself. He had wanted to contribute but had never found the chance. He'd grown close to Phira and as a result ended up backing most of her ideas rather than thinking up his own. It was a natural thing in feline societies. Most of the time the females ruled with the males deferring to them regularly.

"But that doesn't mean we're their servants,"

Miko's mind was ablaze with revelation and self-evaluation.

A question occurred to him.

"Hera?" he said, startling her out of some thoughts of her own.

She turned to look at him. Mikos suddenly found himself wondering if Hera and Calix were related somehow. Their coloring was similar and shared many of the same patterns. Hera's orange hood didn't cover as much of her face, and she was slimmer than Calix. Calix kept herself well groomed, while Hera had a more unkept appearance. Hera was also much older than Calix. Hera's impatient voice snapped him back to this moment.

"Yes? What is it?"

"You mentioned the council will deal with Dahlia. What is the plan you have for that?"

"Who's... Dahlia?" she replied impatiently.

Mikos hissed quietly and flicked his tail in annoyance, almost daring Hera to notice.

"The new stray Hera, the one that was abandoned. She's pregnant, and by the looks of it will be giving birth very soon"

"Is she? I hadn't heard that, just that there was a new one to deal with."

"To deal with?"

Miko's tail whipped back and forth more forcefully.

"Do you think so little of your fellow strays, Hera?"

"What would you know about being a stray Mikos?"

"She's got me there," he admitted to himself, *"still."*

"So, there is no plan for the council to discuss?"

Hera stopped in agitation, turned to him, sat down and glared right into his eyes.

"What would you have us discuss Mikos?"

"I would have us discuss ways to help Dahlia."

"How? What can we do? It's way too late to attempt to get her safely ensconced with one of the humans. With a storm coming none of the places safe from those murderous beasts is usable."

"Well..."

Hera raised her voice, yowling at him.

"Well what Mikos! Should we all band together to fight off those two wretches!? You've seen what they are capable of. How many of us would have to die to save this Dahlia and her brood, half of which probably won't live to see a year anyhow."

"They deserve the chance!" He howled back at her. His head low, ears laid flat as, anticipating an attack.

"WE ALL DO!" she shouted over him.

She positioned her body as if to strike. To forcibly subdue him. He saw it coming and prepared himself.

"This is my chance" he thought, *"to make myself heard"*

THUMP

They both leapt into the air at his new threat. Mikos landed a couple feet away, back humped hair fluffed, presenting as large and threatening a profile as possible for this assailant. His heart thumped in his chest as he looked at what had jumped in on their argument.

"A rock?" he said aloud.

He looked up and saw Hera mirroring his posture a few feet away. She too was coming to the realization that they had been interrupted by a rock. A thrown rock. Which meant

A loud shout from a human echoed off the trees around them.

Hera and Mikos linked up and silently scurried away. It was never a good idea to hang around angry humans.

"Come on Mikos," Hera said, more calmly and gently. "The Council is waiting"

Mikos followed, deciding not to press Hera further.

As they trotted away, he glanced back at the way they had come, the beginnings of an idea, a plan, taking shape in his mind.

"Won't Calix be surprised." he thought to himself, then turned and followed after Hera.

Chapter Fifteen

Calix

CALIX, CURRENTLY BACKED UP against a bush, strained and squeezed to eke out a few more drops from her bladder. She was thankful this part of the plan was over with, and that no one caught her at it, there were going to be A LOT of territorial disputes once this was over with.

"A little something for the council to deal with" she purred to herself in satisfaction.

She sat down to rest a bit, the tip of her tail flicking around in satisfaction as her imagination spun out scenarios of Hera desperately trying to quiet a cacophony of arguments between everyone who assumed Calix's "exploits" indicated some significant change was coming.

After a little while, she sighed inwardly and got up.

"Ok" she thought to herself *"time to do the hard part"*

In her mind, this was the most terrifying aspect of their plan. If she failed here, she and Nyke might have done nothing more than invite a more savage and brutal run through Poros than Elmax and Ajax's usual.

That would not be good, not good at all.

Yet here she was doubting her ability to pull it off. She wasn't sure she had the right temperament for this negotiation, but Nyke had insisted it had to be her. He'd get the help they needed in getting everything else set up, but Nyke had been absolutely certain he would fail, and she would succeed in this one part.

"Come on Calix." she said to herself, trying to find her confidence, "you can do this."

She'd faced down scratching Elmax and Ajax!

Pissed right in their faces!

But a short little conversation. A simple request. That, THAT had her wanting to fluff out her fur and run away.

She moved on, wandering vaguely in the direction she needed to go, trying to build up the courage to do this thing, or at least decide on how she was going to start doing this thing.

"Of all the times to get an itchy tail." she said to herself in disappointment.

She kept walking, trying to understand why she was so afraid, to understand what it was about herself that THIS, of all things, was the most challenging part of the plan for her.

She shook her head a little.

"I don't get it" she thought to herself, *"It's a solid plan Nyke and I have come up ..."*

"Nyke and I" she said out loud and let out a little chirp.

The words reverberated through her mind, ushering in some clarity.

Calix and Nyke were a team, a team that didn't trust others, especially when it came to needing help. Calix had been on her own for so long with Nyke as her only true compatriot that the thought of trusting anyone else to help in this situation terrified her. She could use others, yes, but trust them? Not so much. The truth though, was that the cats couldn't deal with the threat of Elmax and Ajax on their own, not even if all of them banded together to fight. That's one of the reasons the council had set up a watch and warning system and then considered the matter settled.

It hadn't been enough for Calix or Nyke. They'd come up with a plan and waited for an opportunity to enact it. Even started doing prep work with some of the other cats who'd become dissatisfied with the council's reticence. But it was a plan that needed outside help to succeed, and it was that need that had her scared. The fact that they had to rely on someone other than themselves, no guarantees against betrayal. What a terrifying prospect, having to ask for help, but having absolutely nothing to fall back on if they were denied it.

She understood her fear now and knew what she had to do. Which was good because, to her surprise, she was where she needed to be.

Calix blinked as she recognized the white wooden gate, plants flanking either side. She laughed at herself in amusement.

"Guess my paws knew the way of it even when I did not."

"What's that now?" A deep voice rumbled from the other side of the gate. "Calix? Is that you?"

Calix leapt up and perched herself on the top of the gate, looking down into the small, enclosed garden.

Barnabus, a great big shaggy mountain of a dog, lay there, half in the sun, half out. Curled up on his flank and nestled down in his thick fur slept Anthos, a young cat sporting thin scars across his body and missing half his tail. His only reaction to Calix's presence was to swivel an ear in her direction for a brief moment.

Barnabus, however, was looking right at her.

"What brings you here Calix?"

Calix had put a tremendous amount of thought into how to ask what she needed to ask. She'd replayed potential conversations in her mind through thousands of iterations. She'd plotted out and come up with convincing replies to every conceivable reason Barnabus could come up with for turning her down.

As she sat there on the gate, looking down at him, all that shit flew out of her mind like a spooked flock of pigeons.

Before she could even recapture them and begin her much rehearsed monologue, she felt her mouth open and heard a single sentence spill out of it.

"Hey Barnabus, how'd you like a bite at Elmax and Ajax?"

Anthos thumped onto the ground and looked around in confusion as Barnabus shot to his feet and moved toward Calix.

"Can we do it right now, or do I have to wait?" Barnabus growled.

In response Calix just looked at him. Her ears twitched forward as a fierce and predatory sparkle entered her eyes, matching Barnabus's enthusiasm.

"Scratch you Nyke, you KNEW this is how it would go down" Calix thought to herself, *"of course you scratching did."*

She jumped down and took a seat in front of Barnabus. She looked him in the eyes and heard the cunning in her own voice as she said,

"You'll have to wait a little bit. You see, I'm going to lead them straight to you."

Barnabus could barely contain his excitement and she explained their plan to him.

Chapter Sixteen

Dahlia

DAHLIA WOKE IN CONFUSION. Tiny pinpricks of pain had brought her to consciousness. Sparking around in her mind like a flight of fireflies, demanding attention.

She opened her eyes to see what kept nipping at her. Four tiny objects were cuddled up to her, one suckling. She could just make them out in the darkness.

"Darkness?" she thought to herself. *"When did it get dark?"*

Then the memories came flooding back in.

Mikos, Calix, Nyke, everything that had happened began to swim into her awareness.

"Nyke!"

She looked around for him as the memory of their conversation came back to her. He'd mentioned a threat and she'd demanded he tell her about it, but then.

One of the tiny forms snuggled up to her mewed and drew her attention.

Dahlia shifted her body a little and began cleaning the restless one. Its head bobbed around as she licked, and it began to shuffle its way over its siblings. Soon enough it found a nipple to latch onto and quieted down. Its jostling had awakened one of the others who then also began searching for an exposed nipple to latch on to.

Dahlia went back to trying to remember what had happened, and how it had happened.

Within seconds of her saying "Tell Me.", two things had happened.

She'd thrown up all the food they'd given her, and then gone into labor.

She was curious as to why she didn't remember much after that.

Flashes of pain and amazement mixed together in her memory to form a fog through which she had difficulty discerning the timeline of events. She didn't even know how long it had taken, though obviously long enough for the sun to go down.

Her last two kittens stirred and began moving themselves to a position from which they could get some milk.

Still gathering her thoughts together, Dahlia stretched her body out to make it easier for them to find. Soon all four sets of tiny paws were kneading at her while her kittens fed.

"The threat, the threat, the threat" she repeated to herself, as her eyes began to close. Trying to remind herself that she needed to stay conscious. She remembered the labor. Remembered the feel of her body as it tried to squeeze itself into a ball from the inside. Remembered the feeling of each of her children passing from her body out into the world.

The scent of her labor still permeated the air.

"Nyke said something about the scent." she recalled aloud.

She remembered Nyke trying to fill her in even as her labor continued, but she'd been a little too busy to focus on what he was saying.

"Amazing you have remembered that much." said a voice out of the darkness.

Dahlia, startled, hissed forcefully, then calmed as she realized who had spoken.

"Calix?"

"Oh, you remember me too? I'm flattered."

"Wha..." she began.

"Was Nyke able to tell you the plan, or at least your part of it?"

"He was able to relay most of it to me."

"Where is Nyke?" she thought to herself. She must have looked around for him because Calix interrupted her search.

"Nyke's off making other preparations just now, though everything important is already in place"

"Important to what?" she asked, then she gave her head a little shake, "The plan, obviously."

Calix seemed to realize she wasn't completely in charge of herself yet.

"It's all right," she said gently, "you've just spent several hours giving birth to four adorable kittens, one of them a mini version of yourself no less. I'll go over everything again for you really

quick so that you understand what you need to do, or rather what you need to NOT do."

She looked at Calix numbly, "Not do?"

"Right, Ok," Calix said "Not completely here yet I see. Well, I'm sorry for this."

Before she could say anything else, Calix stalked up to her. Dahlia's eyes widened as they met Calix's. Widened even further when she noticed Calix's ears were folded all the way down, ready to fight. She'd barely had time to register this when Calix roared a full-throated challenge right in her face. It was loud, it was forceful, it was unacceptable.

Dahlia's mind became clearer as a surge of energy coursed through her body. She picked herself up, ignoring the frustrated cries of her kittens, interrupted at their meal. She placed herself between them and Calix.

"HOW DARE Y.." she began but stopped herself.

Calix's posture was completely different than a moment before. She sat cleaning her paws casually as if she hadn't just threatened Dahlia with violence.

She looked up from her grooming, the tip of her tail flicking back and forth in amusement.

"Welcome back, how was giving birth?"

The humor relaxed Dahlia a little.

"Was that really necessary?" she asked and looked down at her kittens. "You interrupted their mealtime."

"Probably not," Calix said, "that was more for me than for you honestly. May I ask, how much of the plan do you remember"

Dahlia turned her mind inward, working at finding Nyke's voice amid the events of the past few hours. It wasn't easy, but bits and pieces began to put themselves together.

Nyke and Calix had a plan, a plan for dealing with two dogs who terrorized pretty much every other living thing in Poros, even some of the humans. They were going to use their greed for violence against them and lure them into a trap, one set at a preselected location. They had thought up this plan long ago, just never had the one thing that gave them the opportunity to set it. The bait, aka the birth of a litter of kittens that couldn't be hidden by the council in time. The one thing that always made Elmax and Ajax leave their home to go hunting was the scent of kittens on the wind. Nothing else reliably brought them out.

"I remember enough to know you're using us as bait." Dahlia said coldly.

"Ah, there it is," Calix said, "technically true, but not really. Your scent is the bait, but we've no intention of letting that trail lead back to you. That's why it's so important for you to understand what you're NOT to do."

Dahlia looked at Calix, she remembered the instructions now, even understood the reasoning behind them. They still left her feeling uneasy.

"I'm to not move my kittens, no matter what, unless directed to do so by you or Nyke."

As she said this Nyke entered through the tunnel of leaves, looked at Calix and gave a slight nod. Calix turned her head back to her.

"That's correct, it is very important that you stay hidden. Also though, we're not going to leave you alone, Nyke will be here with you the whole time. I know it's not easy Dahlia, but I'm asking you to trust us in this"

Dahlia wasn't entirely sure, but she was exhausted and drained and couldn't think of any other options. All she wanted right now was to stay with her little ones and sleep. She dipped her head in acknowledgement.

"I will trust you." she said wearily.

"Thank you," Calix said, "Now move aside please, I need to roll around in those leaves for a moment if you don't mind."

Chapter Seventeen

Mikos

NETTLES AND LEAVES BRUSHED his fur as he followed Hera down a slight slope toward the council's favorite meeting place. Lost in his own thoughts, his surroundings barely registered on his consciousness.

"Are you listening to me Mikos!?"

Mikos looked forward and noticed Hera had stopped and was looking back at him, glaring at him really.

"Yes, of course," he managed, "What else do I need to know before we get there?"

Hera stared at him a bit longer, so still that Mikos was beginning to wonder if she was ok or if some terror was creeping up behind them.

"I'll start over," she said and turned to continue downward.

"I'll start over" Mikos mimicked quietly, but then hurried to catch up to her.

Her voice picking up again as he came back within range

"... not to get too enamored of Calix's rebellious streak. "She" has ideas about the Council's reason for existence that fall outside the original intent and purpose of its formation..."

Hera always made the "she" sound like an insult or something beyond belief when talking about Calix. It was a petty, spiteful thing to do and one of the reasons Calix disliked Hera so much. No one ever called her out on it though.

"We all think of it as Hera being Hera and let it go at that, a pity." Mikos thought to himself as Hera droned on.

"... and don't get me started on that weird relationship 'she' and Nyke have. Are they mates? Cohorts? What? They behave as if they are family but work together as if they are a single unit and every cat on the island is their child. It's not natural Mikos..."

"Why did Calix say I had a plan?" That's what Mikos was curious about.

He had one now but hadn't before. Had Calix planned that? Was Nyke in on it? He wanted to help them, but what if what he had come up with didn't work well with whatever they had planned?

"I need to talk to Phira." he said aloud.

"You say something?" Hera said. "Never mind, where was I? Oh yes, you must prepare yourself Mikos. The council isn't in the business of..."

Mikos ignored Hera and returned to his own thoughts, reflecting on his and Phira's friendship, wondering why Hera never felt the need to call them "unnatural". No matter, he was sure she would help him if he could just have a few moments to explain his idea to her before he presented it to the Council.

He was sure she would see the merit in it, and maybe even know the best way to sell it to the Council. Phira was good at that. She'd often run things by him first, to assure he'd vote her way. She'd even incorporate any suggestions he made. She'd sometimes change them up a little to make them seem more "palatable to the council", but she always assured him it was his input that helped her decide how best to present it. Even when the presentation sounded completely different from what he had said.

They made a good team, him and Phira. Something Hera was saying caught his attention.

"... finite number of resources Mikos. We can't go around dedicating time and energy to every poor soul that gets dropped off here. Life can be cruel, and we need to accept that, you need to accept..."

"Do we though?" he thought, memories swirling up to show him snapshots of their interactions.

The question popped into his mind because he had found himself thinking of how he was going to describe his plan to Phira, found himself trying to think of a way to spin it so that she would present it as HE wanted it to be presented rather than whatever she had in mind.

That's when it hit him.

They did make a good team. For Phira. Even now, when he had come up with a plan all his own, Miko's first thoughts were of how Phira would present it to the council. Not how he would present it, but how she would.

Another thought smacked him between the eyes.

"I've never actually presented anything to the council." He was a little bit shocked to realize this.

After that one the realizations just kept coming. He looked at his and Phira's interactions with fresh whiskers. She'd never really used his ideas and input, not once. It seems he was a guaranteed vote to her, nothing more. Everyone else believed this about their relationship. A wave of embarrassment swept through him, making his fur stand up a little.

Then shame, anger and finally loneliness came in quick succession. Mikos decided to circle back and grab ahold of that anger.

"I'll sort out this stuff about Phira later," he thought, *"I've got to plan what I'm going to say to the Council"*

Oblivious to Miko's inner turmoil, Hera kept on talking. "... expect anyone to back whatever this plan of yours is Mikos. Not even Phira. Nobody wants to get involved in dealing with those two anymore than we already have. It's a nasty business..."

Mikos sharpened his resolve and tuned out Hera completely. He had a statement to plan, and he was excited and terrified by the prospect all at once. They moved on, Hera talking at him the entire time, Mikos turned completely inward. Eventually they made it to the meeting place and a new voice brought him out of his reverie.

"... Well, Mikos? Going to take your place or not?"

Mikos snapped his attention back outward. Hera and the rest of the council were arrayed around him, all of them staring. Phira seemed to be looking at him weirdly, as if she knew the turmoil his mind had gone through thanks to a single joke from Calix.

He knew what Calix had been doing now, taunting him. Taunting him for pretending to be more than he was. A lonely old cat, trading usefulness for feigned friendship. Wasn't that just a burr on the back of the neck.

"Yes, of course", he said and moved to join the council meeting.

He caused a slight stir when he intentionally passed Phira and found a spot farther away from her rather than lounging right next to her as was his habit.

Tail flicks and ear twitches filled the air with quiet thumps and whispers of movement.

Mikos chose a place exactly opposite Phira. As he sat, he lifted his face and looked directly into her eyes with all the courage he could muster. He saw realization dawn on her.

"That's right," he thought toward her in self-satisfaction, *"your tool is claiming independence".*

All she did was hold his gaze for a moment, and then look to the side. Not even a blink to commemorate their time together. Mikos almost fell into a sense of loss, letting it sweep him away, when Hera's official voice boomed through the council.

"With everyone gathered, I hereby call this Council to order!"

"Seconded!" someone shouted.

"The council is now in session!"

Hera stepped forward.

"As this is a session specially called to address an issue that has long plagued our island, I move that we go straight to the business at hand and let the member who called this Council speak!"

Several voices seconded this motion and it passed. Hera turned to Phira.

"I yield to Phira."

Phira stepped forward, she looked at them each in turn, all save Mikos.

"Council members," she said, "I've called us together to discuss a threat to the peace of our community. You know who I'm speaking of. Too long have these two terrorized the stability of our lives here. Threatened to pull everything we've built apart. Their unwillingness to abide by our treaties and agreements puts us all in great danger. So much so that we all often move about with caution, wary of our own homes."

Phira turned to Mikos then, returning the challenge he'd presented her with, daring him to move against what she planned. Nothing could have prepared him for what she said next.

"Calix and Nyke have upset the balance we strive so hard to maintain too many times."

Phira's eyes remained locked with his as if she wanted to watch the weight of her words hit him. In shocked silence he guessed what was coming next.

"They have repeatedly shown that they are unwilling to help keep the peace of Poros. I move that we banish them to the interior for the remainder of their lives, upon pain of death!"

"It seems Phira has plans of her own." Mikos spat quietly.

Chapter Eighteen

Mikos

FOR PERHAPS THE FIRST time in his life Mikos stared down another cat. The events of the day had challenged him in ways he couldn't have anticipated. Individually those events had been small.

His day to watch the quay.

Another cat abandoned by her human caretakers.

Meeting Dahlia and realizing she was very pregnant.

Calix jumping into the water to save a cat she'd only just met.

How he'd foolishly thought they'd both been lost because of Nyke's reaction, not realizing that Nyke was simply trying to draw the attention of some humans.

Hera flat out lying to Calix about the council's intentions.

Realizing that Calix had known the lie would come before she'd even voiced it.

Mikos's mind had been a chaotic swirl of revelation and self-evaluation, one he'd barely started to get a handle on. He'd barely had time to process the shock of seeing the truth about his relationship with Phira when she'd made her play to banish Calix and Nyke. That act had focused the chaos of his mind. Sharpened his focus down to the point of a claw. He was angry, enraged even, but it was cold anger, one that fueled rather than consumed.

So, he stared Phira down and waited.

He had always liked Calix and Nyke. He tended to think of them as tricksters occasionally getting one over on Hera or the council at large, but rarely taking matters seriously.

"I did them a disservice, to think so little of them." he thought. Looking back at his memories of them and their antics with new awareness. One that wasn't quite as clouded by his status as one of the few cats with actual human caretakers. One of the few who had a human home to retire into whenever he wished.

Calix and Nyke worked for survival, worked for those abandoned or banished by the council and its edicts. Worked toward solutions rather than stopgap actions.

Mikos remembered all the faces he'd seen come and go. The faces of those who eked out a living on the fringes of their little society here. He remembered the ones taken by Elmax and Ajax. Remembered the ones given to disease and starvation in the wilderness.

Remembered the ones scraping by on the garbage the strays blessed by the council wouldn't touch. They'd barely registered with him before. Just faces caught at a distance, aways around for a few weeks or months, then gone as if they'd never existed. Calix and Nyke worked to help all of them, though not always successfully.

Mikos found himself gaining a measure of respect for Nyke and Calix that he hadn't had before. He understood why Phira and Hera wanted them gone. They upset the balance the council struggled to maintain. The balance that kept the humans sweeping through and disappearing as many as they could catch. A true act of irony since most of them were in the position they were because of human actions. Like Dahlia, cared for when it was convenient, cast aside when it wasn't.

Like Callix and Nyke. Tolerated as long as they didn't get too many feline hackles up, but now becoming an inconvenience.

"Why now?" he wondered as Phira attempted to drill into him with her gaze.

"Something to do with Elmax and Ajax?"

Even as he asked the question a possibility came to him, making his anger fluoresce into fury.

They USED Elmax and Ajax! Every unsanctioned litter, every accident, every lone stray hunting on the fringes looking for a place to belong. They were targets for Elmax and Ajax. Elmax and Ajax helped manage the population in a way that was convenient to the council. Helped keep them from having to find food for extra mouths. Kept them from having to do anything but accept what the humans gave them and lay around in the sun.

"Do Calix and Nyke know?" he asked himself.

"Of course, they know." came the reply. *"They've always known."*

Mikos continued to meet Phira's gaze.

He felt shame for himself, at how complacent he'd been most of his life. Unwilling and unable to see the reality before him, but he had an idea now and the will to see it through.

He became aware of others gathered around. A good chunk of the population of Poros in fact.

"Have they been there this whole time?"

Phira blinked, slowly

A quick wetting of the eyes, but everyone who saw it knew what it signified. Knew that the contest of wills had been settled.

Phira looked away and yawned, feigning disinterest.

"Well, Mikos," she finally said, "you look as if you'd like to address the council."

Commotion about them as she spoke betrayed the truth of the situation. No-one had ever seen Mikos win a challenge like that, or even make one. Mikos sat silently, held her stare, he wasn't falling for that one. A few more moments, and then miraculously, Phira backed down. She lowered her body, stretching it out on the ground, yielding the floor to him, tail twitching back and forth like a whip. It was her final attempt to intimidate him.

It didn't work.

Mikos stood and looked toward Hera.

"I have a counter motion, but I would like to address this council and everyone else assembled here before I present it."

Hera looked like she was about to object when...

"I move he be allowed to speak" said Sable, a dark thick furred cat from the lowest terrace.

"Seconded!" "Seconded" "SECONDED!"

The three who had seconded looked to each other, nodding.

Hera had no choice now.

"Ayes?"

The vote was unanimous, save Hera. Surprisingly, Phira had said "aye".

"Motion passes, Mikos you have our attention, but make it quick"

"It will take as long as it takes," he said back to her.

He moved to position himself at the center of the group.

He looked around at all those gathered.

Took a deep breath.

And began to speak.

Chapter Nineteen

Nyke

NYKE HEAD BUTTED CALIX warmly as she returned to their lair.

"Well, it's a nursery now, for better or worse" he thought to himself.

Calix returned his greeting, her head brushing up against his chin and along his neck. Breathing in their commingled scents brought him some comfort and relaxation. A reaffirmation of their friendship, their dedication to one another.

"How is she?" Calix asked.

"Sh-sh-she is well, if a bit t-t-tired"

"And the kittens?"

"F-f-four, all healthy, b-b-by the look of it."

A sigh of relief escaped Calix.

"Small victories."

"I d-d-don't believe she's decided to n-n-name them after m-m-me yet."

Any other cat would have paused to look at Nyke to judge his tone, Calix however,

"I'll be sure to petition her to do just that."

They both flicked their tails in amusement.

As much as he loved their banter though, it was time to attend to serious matters.

"Is everything r-r-ready?"

"As ready as we can make it. Oh scratch it Nyke, I'm so nervous I'm tempted to pray to that Bastet Dahlia mentioned."

"It's a g-g-good plan. It will work"

"I do hope so."

Nyke sniffed the air. A nearby storm had been heard and scented on the wind but not yet felt. Rain clouds had rolled over the mainland, but so far none had touched the island. That was good.

"Looks like it will all b-b-be over b-b-by the time any s-s-storm arrives."

"Thank goodness for that."

"What is left to b-b-be done?"

Calix gave him a brief rundown of everything she'd been able to get done as well as the tasks left to be managed. All the prep work had been done. Now it was just a matter of waiting for Elmax and Ajax to leave their home and start hunting, which they would do as soon as their human went down for the night.

The council meeting pricked his curiosity though. *"I didn't think they'd get it together enough to gather tonight"* he thought. *"Interesting that they did."*

He kind of wanted to see what went down.

"C-c-can you k-k-keep an eye on them? I want to see if I c-c-can catch that c-c-council meeting."

"Of course," Calix replied, "besides, I need to go cover myself in the scent of all that newborn stuff anyway."

"Remind her that she needs to s-s-stay in p-p-place please"

"Will do" Calix said as she disappeared into the bush.

Nyke went off in search of the Council meeting. There were a few possible locations and he worried slightly that he might not find it in time to learn anything of their intentions.

"No matter," he thought to himself, *"the outcome of the meeting won't really affect our plans for tonight."*

"Tonight" was quickly approaching. The sun had already dipped below the horizon and the world around him was already trading its color for deepening shades of gray. Motion to the left caught his attention. He paused to look, head up, waiting to see if the movement was friend of foe. A cat named Fluff emerged from some high grass.

"Hey Nyke, you going to the meeting?"

Nyke twitched his ears in the affirmative.

"D-d-do you know where it is b-b-being held?"

"Yeah, down by the trough, a lot of cats are going. Supposedly some big motion is going to be made."

"Mind if I t-t-tag along with you?"

"Not at all."

Fluff resumed his walk toward the trough, breaking into a trot. Nyke trotted up next to him and they moved on together. Quietly and quickly.

As it happened, they arrived at the outskirts of the trough area just as Mikos and Hera were taking their places among the council.

Several cats sitting on the outskirts glanced at them, intoned greetings, or ignored them. Nyke nodded where it was appropriate, but otherwise focused on the proceedings. He heard them declare the council in session, but was drifting off a little, lost in his own thoughts. He registered that Phira had begun talking about some threat, which turned his mind to Elmax and Ajax and what they had planned for them.

A loud gasp brought him out of his reverie.

He glanced over to find Fluff looking at him with an expression of shock in his eyes.

"What?"

Then his ears caught up with his mind as the words he'd heard but not registered filtered into his consciousness.

"They have repeatedly shown that they are unwilling to help keep the peace of Poros. I move that we banish them to the interior for the remainder of their lives!"

That's what Phira had said, talking about him and Calix, not Elmax and Ajax.

His ears went cold and folded down upon his head. He looked around, noticed all of the cats nearby noticing he was there and whispering to each other.

"Scratch it Nyke, I don't know what to..." Fluff was saying to him.

"It is ok Fluff," he said. "We've enough f-f-friends that it won't p-p-pass. This is performative."

"Anyway," Fluff replied and stood, "I've got to go get in position for what you and Calix have planned."

The reminder pulled him back to the moment.

"Yes, he's right. This still won't affect our plans" Nyke thought, *"we can deal with this after."*

That thought calmed him considerably. Calmed him enough that he caught sight of the silent showdown between Mikos and Phira. Calmed him down enough to realize how novel this development was.

Nyke sat on his haunches and watched as Mikos 'Mikos!?' challenged Phira and then declared his desire to speak to those assembled. He kept quiet as the motion was seconded, lest his distinctive stutter alert Hera and Phira to his presence among those watching.

"Scratch and claw, but it is good to see him stand up to those two!"

Nyke's tail swished in satisfaction as Mikos took his place to speak to the Council and everyone assembled. He looked calm, collected, ready.

"All of you know me." he started. "I have a home. I have humans who take care of me, feed me, provide for me. I am one of the few on this island that has never wanted for anything, never NEEDED for anything. Every possible need I could have, is seen to."

"Stop rubbing it in Mikos!" a voice in the crowd shouted.

"Seconded" came a muffled shout, to everyone's amusement.

Mikos continued.

"Alright, I get it, I hope you get it too. I do not know what it is to live the way in which most of you live. But I do see it. I see it every day during watches, I see it in the actions of this council, I see it in the territories and activities of all of you as you work to keep yourselves fed, work to keep yourselves alive."

Nyke found himself entranced.

"You're the successful ones!" he continued. "You're the ones who have survived, you're the ones who've received the Council's blessing to take part in sharing the food humans provide for us. To take part in the little bit of protection and care they afford us."

"What are you getting at Mikos?" Nyke thought.

"Not everyone is so lucky though, right? Remember Taffy, Saf, Rynar, Smoke, Patch, Lightfoot..."

The list of names went on for a bit, some of them names Nyke had completely forgotten about. He found himself shocked that Mikos remembered all of them.

Every single name belonged to a cat that had died, succumbed to starvation, disease, hardship, or been victims of Elmax and Ajax.

There were so many, the silence of the crowd seemed to deepen as Mikos listed every name he knew. When he was done, he paused and took the time to look every other council member in the eyes, Hera turned her gaze away from him. Many, though, returned his stare and offered blinks of affection, understanding, and respect. Even Phira.

"Odd" thought Nyke.

After the council, Mikos swept his gaze over the assembled crowd and began again.

"They suffered and paid the price because we have bought into a fantasy. The council has existed for so long and done as it does for so long that we stopped questioning its actions or refining its purpose. We've used it, we've relied on it, to decide who gets to survive and who doesn't. Who starves, and who gets to eat. Whose kittens get to live and who's get sacrificed to those beasts at the top of the hill."

Nyke couldn't tear his eyes away as Mikos began to pace before them.

"We tell ourselves that what this council does is what is best for the survival of us all. That the gifts of food and safety come from the council's benevolence and wisdom. Why? Because it has always been that way!"

"But we have forgotten the most important thing. You and I, we are not at all different. Every one of us is in the same position whether we choose to acknowledge it or not."

Nyke watched with pride as Mikos turned to face down Phira and Hera as he said this. They watched him with unreadable expressions. Clearly both understood what he was about to say next.

"It is not the council that grants us the ability to survive. It is the humans who make this possible. We cannot survive without them. Their food, their shelters, their sufferance. All of us who live here live because humans make it possible. Humans, NOT the Council. For as long as I have been here the council has been the link between humanity and our society, but we've grown complacent. We've grown complacent in facing threats, grown complacent in fulfilling our function as the safeguard of stability for all of us. We've dropped the mantel left by humans, the one they ignore after they've given us food and washed their hands of us. Many have suffered because of this, and our response tonight is to try and banish the only two cats that seem to care about safeguarding every life on the island!"

The assembled cats shifted and mumbled to each other.

"I say it's unconscionable and unacceptable, and while we sit here bickering and complacent, THEY came up with a plan to deal with Elmax and Ajax!"

Mikos shifted his attention back to the crowd.

"I have a plan on how WE can help Calix, if you'd only listen for a moment. I don't care if the council agrees, I don't need them, I need all of you!"

Everyone sat silently, waiting for what came next.

"Will you hear me out?"

"Aye!" The first shout came from Sable. With her broken, withered front leg, she knew of suffering.

Her shout was joined by others, a cacophony of "ayes" sounded from around the hill.

Nyke wanted to stay and hear Miko's plan, but something else had caught his attention.

A lone howl, echoing in the darkness.

Ajax, testing the wakefulness of his human.

Nyke shivered and hurried off to make preparations and check on Dahlia.

It wouldn't be long now.

Chapter Twenty

Interlude

NYKE TROTTED AWAY FROM the Council meeting. He wanted to stay and listen to Miko's idea, but hearing Ajax's probing howl on the wind told him he didn't have the time. Thinking this reminded him of a short exchange he and Calix had had, months ago, about the nature of time.

"Time is such a fickle thing," Calix had said, *"we either have way too much of it or not nearly enough. It's a rare moment when we have just the right amount. Isn't that weird?"*

Nyke had thought about it for a while and eventually countered with,

"I -think that observation is m-m-more a c-c-commentary on us than t-t-time."

Calix had looked away without saying anything more, her way of agreeing with him.

Remembering the exchange in the wake of what he'd just witnessed with Mikos reminded him of one of the things he appreciated and loved most about Calix.

She always gave him time to, not just speak, but think before he spoke. For all her quick wit and clawing humor, she often waited patiently for him to formulate what he wanted to say or how he wanted to respond in any conversation.

He'd asked her about it once, to thank her for putting up with him, and her reply had cemented his affection and loyalty to her. She'd not even made a big deal of it, simply turning her head away and saying softly,

"Nyke, I value our friendship, your companionship and most of all, I value you. You've no need to thank me for listening to you on your own terms, it requires no effort on my part, so there is nothing for me to put up with, as you say."

His love and respect for her soared every time he remembered those words. He also knew what had called up the memory this time.

Mikos, she'd never tried to tell him how Phira was using him, just treated him like she would any friend, and waited to see if he'd gain the confidence to see the truth for himself. That was Calix. Nyke was a better planner, he could admit that, but Calix knew cats, he envied that ability sometimes, but only sometimes.

Another howl tugged on his awareness, cutting off abruptly.

"A reminder, his human is still awake then," Nyke scolded himself, *"so much to do, gate first, then Barnabus..."*

With a list of things to do Nyke spared one last thought for Calix's observations of time and hoped he hadn't just spent too much of it in satisfying his curiosity.

Dahlia heard the howl cut off and wondered what it indicated.

One of her little ones let out a high-pitched mew, distracting her.

She leaned down and began cleaning its head and face, which only made it mew louder and start squirming. As she continued licking it squirmed its way over to her belly, found a nipple and began feeding, purring contentedly to itself. Its paws began kneading, tiny claws extending and retracting, leaving brief pin pricks of pain.

The other three woke up and the process repeated itself until all she could do was stretch out her body and let them suckle. Which gave her entirely too much time to think.

She'd wanted to curse Bastet, that awful tom, her mother, her humans. She hadn't wanted kittens, but Bastet had foisted them on her anyway.

"Not that I don't care about them," she said out loud, "but why me? Oh Bastet, you spiteful goddess, why toy with me?"

She lifted her head and contemplated their little bodies.

She would put her life on the line for them. She'd realized that right off the bat. She knew that wasn't always the case, but for her it was true. *"Scratch it all."*

She moved her mind on to other things. To Nyke and Calix. She wasn't entirely sure she trusted their plan. It was clever, to be sure, but even as she'd watched Calix roll around in the leaves she'd given birth on so she could make herself more convincing as bait, it occurred to her that she should make her own backup plan.

"I should at least find a place to escape to, should it be needed" she thought.

She looked at her kittens again, thinking. After a moment she uttered a single word to herself.

"Yes"

Dahlia picked herself up, dislodging her kittens, who'd mostly fallen asleep in the middle of eating.

She used her nose to nudge them together into a cuddled-up ball. When she was satisfied that they'd be warm and comfortable Dahlia turned around and exited through the tunnel of leaves.

Wandering off in search of a backup space, someplace she could stash her little ones where a dog's snout couldn't get to them, no matter what.

All was quiet and still, not a single breeze sang its melody into the night.

Considering all her time at sea, Dahlia should have noticed and recognized what that could mean, but she had other concerns and so the calm didn't even register.

Something sailed out of the rectangle of light and smacked him right in the forehead, interrupting his howl.

He looked down at it curiously.

"Chew?" he said.

His jaws clamped down on the empty beer can and he began chewing on it. The can crumpled between his teeth.

He felt a slight sting in his mouth and dropped the can, tasting his own blood. He knew enough to know what that tasted like.

"No chew, no chew, no chew".

He grew bored and began wandering the perimeter of their fence again. Following the scents, marking some places, skipping others.

He came to the place Calix had confronted them. Smelled the still strong scent of her urine all over the fence.

"Calix!" he barked "Calix Calix Calix!"

Then he let out a long loud howl.

He saw Elmax's ears pick up as he neared the end of it, but then sank back down when a door swung open, and their human shouted at them again.

Ajax continued his patrol, mumbling "Calix, Calix, Calix, Calix" to himself quietly.

Lucky sat on his tree branch and watched Elmax and Ajax. He hated sentry duty. Mandated by the council on rotation, they claimed they chose sentries randomly, but he felt they chose him more often than others. Not that he was one to challenge the council's decisions. Besides, this watch was usually uneventful. 19 nights out of 20, they stayed behind their fence and didn't do a thing. He got to spend a lot of time napping, which really wasn't that bad if he was being honest.

Not tonight though, they seemed intent on getting out as early as they could.

He'd seen what Calix had done earlier, almost fallen out of the tree with laughter at the sight of Calix pissing right in Elmax's face.

Now though, it didn't seem so funny.

Ajax had started testing with howls early.

Lucky knew that once he was able to get out two long howls without being interrupted by their human, they would make a break for it. They'd get themselves across the fence and out on the prowl.

It was Lucky's job to follow them and make as much noise as possible, alerting everyone in range to their presence. He hoped the other sentries were ready, tonight looked like it was going to be a long one.

He looked down as Ajax started another howl, then jumped straight up with a start.

Something had poked him in the back, Hard.

Lucky's body summersaulted and his hind paws came down on thin air.

With a gasp of surprise, he was able to get his front claws in the branch long enough to slow his fall.

His breath huffed out of him as his body hit the ground, but he righted himself quickly, just in time to see magpie dive for him again.

"Hey, knock it off!" he shouted.

He leaped up to take a swipe at it, but it dodged and flew off.

Lucky chased the bird for a little bit before remembering his duty to watch for Ajax and Elmax to escape their enclosure.

With a sigh he gave up on the magpie and headed back.

He was walking down a path toward his tree when one of Ajax's howls trailed off, not with an abrupt cut off, but with a finishing of his breath. In his altercation with the magpie, Lucky had no idea if this was the first or second howl.

He continued toward his tree warily, listening for a second howl from Ajax, wondering if he'd missed it.

He got his answer a few seconds later. The rustling of the brush father up the path made him pull up short and watch. His eyes grew wide in fear as that rustling turned into Ajax, sprinting toward him at full speed.

Lucky turned and fled, making for the nearest tree.

Chapter Twenty-One

Mikos

HE'D DELIVERED HIS IDEA to the Council and the others who'd assembled to watch the proceedings.

He'd explained in detail what he thought they should do, and to his surprise, they'd agreed to do it. Or rather, enough of them had agreed to do it that all the others decided to go along with it. Which was good, his plan was very simple, but required all of them to pull it off.

"Well, most of us," he thought to himself, watching as two cats approached.

Sable was with him, and together they had already dispatched messengers to reach as many cats as possible and have them come together at Calix and Nyke's little hiding spot. The place where they'd stashed Dahlia.

"She's probably given birth by now," he'd told each of them, "so pass the word, be quiet until it's time."

It could prove disastrous if they startled the new mother into moving her kittens to some unknown location.

Each of the messengers had acknowledged the instructions and then rushed off to spread the word as quickly as possible. All of them could hear Ajax's probing howls, a goad to work as quickly as possible.

Mikos sighed.

He did not want to face the two approaching them, but knew that he had to, if only briefly. He turned to Sable, favoring her with a blink.

"It might be good if you went ahead. You could help organize everyone's placement, keep them spread out just enough to avoid notice but with clear paths to gather."

She dipped her head and blinked in acknowledgement then turned her head, regarding the two cats slowly approaching.

"Don't judge them too harshly Mikos. We are all doing our best to survive in a world created for us by humans. You would do well to be mindful of that."

Mikos gave her a stare, lowering his ears a little, his anger rose up, readied a retort.

In response, Sable lifted up her lame paw and started gently cleaning it. Her leg had been broken by a human, kicking her for no other reason than she had been underfoot and hadn't gotten out of the way quickly enough. It had healed badly and was crooked. By all appearances, any pressure she put on that leg resulted in tremendous pain. Even cleaning it looked to be difficult.

"Please Sable, you've no need to cause yourself pain to make a point. Also though, point taken, I'll talk with them."

Sable blinked again and moved off, sparing soft nods for Hera and Phira, the two who had been approaching.

"What do you want?" he said to them when they were close enough, "come to hijack my plan and turn it into something different?"

He glared at Phira who, after a moment, at least had the grace to look away. It was Hera though, who spoke first.

"There's a part of me Mikos that hopes someday you will come to truly understand the risk your plan will bring on us, but in order for that to happen, you would have to live through something I wouldn't wish on my worst enemy."

"There is risk in any endeavor Hera, my plan mitigates that though, accounts for it..."

Phira drew her ears back and hissed at him...

"That's not what she's talking about you fool, you simple fool!"

"Then what is she talking about? What am I risking?"

"Us, Mikos," Phira said more quietly, "you are risking us."

"I don't take your meaning, if we follow my plan, there should be almost no risk at...."

"YOU risk nothing Mikos, Nothing! You have placed all the risk on us!"

Then Hera found her voice and raged at him.

"You think Elmax and Ajax are dangerous? You think they are the biggest threat we face? You are a fool to believe that Mikos, but I see how you could be blinded. Your speech was good, your list of names lost to those monstrosities was poignant, but the reality Elmax and Ajax might as well be rampaging kittens compared to what the humans can and will do to us if we become an inconvenience to them. That's the risk WE take, not you though, you've got your human home to retire to safely! You play scratch the snake with our lives and you're not even aware of it!"

Mikos found himself caught off guard by her tirade.

"But I... what... I..."

Phira picked up where Hera left off.

"You have no concept of what went on before. The stories passed on to us. Of humans sweeping through the town, scooping up every cat they could get their paws on, none ever seen again. The mass graves, the stench of them. That's the reality we live with Mikos. This world, created by humans, where we can't survive without them, but they barely tolerate us! So many of us abandoned or lost, left to fend for ourselves as best we can. Oh they leave out food, the few that care, but there's the rest Mikos. It is a delicate balance, an uneasy peace. They tolerate us, but make no mistake, the moment we become too much trouble for them we become pests to be exterminated. What you plan tonight might just cross that line. I hope it doesn't, but..."

"This is why you moved to have Calix and Nyke banished?"

"They are troublemakers, they upset everything we work so hard to maintain."

They sat together in silence for a few seconds. Both Hera and Phira seemed tired, defeated. The hard part was, he understood now.

Hera was right, he wasn't at risk. If the humans decided to do something drastic about their population, he would be safe, guarded by his own humans. It had never dawned on him that those like Hera, Phira, Calix and Nyke lived with a constant awareness that humans might decide to end their lives someday.

He felt a wave of sympathy, empathy and sorrow for them, he understood something else about these four though.

"Calix and Nyke work to the same end as you and the council."

Hera and Phira looked up at him, confused.

"The human world is changing, seems to me Calix and Nyke are simply trying to keep up with it. Maybe the council has become so petrified by its rules and ordinances that adapting has become impossible. Consider how you used me, to simply maintain the status quo. I'm pretty sure Calix and Nyke know what humans are capable of, yet they still refuse to live in a world where cruelty like that of Elmax and Ajax goes unchallenged. Why would you deny us minds like that? If humans won't manage us, and we all know they won't, wouldn't you want all sorts contributing to our governance?"

Hera and Phira looked at each other. Their ears had picked up and they had the look of those considering something new for the first time and a long while.

Phira opened her mouth to speak but was cut off by a long loud yowl blanketing the island.

All ears and heads swiveled toward the source of the warning.

"That's Lucky!" Hera exclaimed, "They're out."

She shared a look with Phira then turned to Mikos.

"We're with you, this time…"

"We're going to have to discuss this further though," Phira interjected, "what you've said… Mikos, I'll just say we should take some time to have a long talk."

Mikos pushed his head into her, brushing against the underside of her chin as he moved past.

"I understand now, but I'd still like to talk things out once this is over."

She pushed back on him briefly, signaling her assent and then together, all three of them turned and sprinted toward the rendezvous.

Chapter Twenty-Two

Calix

She stopped as Lucky flew across her field of view at full sprint. His eyes wide, his entire body seemed focused on a single goal, escape. The white blur that followed him a few seconds later gave testament as to why.

"Scratch it all!" Calix swore to herself, "Lucky, all you had to do was stay in the scratch tree! Why they keep putting you on sentry duty, I'll never know"

She needed to think fast. They'd counted on Ajax being the first in line of pursuit, but if Ajax went hearing off after the watch that would leave...

As if on cue Elmax stepped across the path. Moving at a much slower pace he was able to pick up Calix's scent. He stopped, sniffing about, lowered his nose to the ground, sniffed a few more times, then raised his head and looked directly at Calix.

"Calix. How nice of you to bring yourself to us."

"Scratch! scratch! Scratch! Scratch it all!" she thought, her mind racing, *"how do I get Ajax back in...?"*

Then she had it. She looked at Elmax, and in her most terrified voice screeched.

"NO! Don't hurt the kittens!"

It was loud enough that Ajax heard it and he pulled up short with a quick "Kittens?"

Then he turned on his heels and sprinted back toward Elmax, much to the relief of Lucky who made it to a tree and then proceeded to yowl out warning signal.

Calix kept her eye on Elmax, she was a little shocked that that had worked but she wasn't about to question it. She waited and watched, hoping Elmax would do what she needed.

She was about to give up on it when it finally came. Elmax swiveled his head to look at the approaching Ajax. The instant his snout was pointed away from her she turned and ran back down the path for all she was worth. She'd laid such a strong trail of scents down they wouldn't need to see her to follow, and she knew Ajax would pick up the scent instantly.

"As he would have earlier if Lucky hadn't been on the ground right in scratching front of him!" she thought.

True to form, Ajax met up with Elmax and, without slowing, turned to race after Calix.

Calix ran, she had to do her best to make it appear as if she was fleeing in a blind panic, heading for some nondescript place where she felt safe. It was kind of easy, all things considered. The view of a salivating Ajax bearing down on you tended to have that effect.

She raced down the path and down into the structures of the top terrace of Poros proper. She jumped up and raced along fence rails. Hopped up and down and over those contraptions the humans zipped around on. All the while Ajax got closer and closer with Elmax not far behind.

Pausing on the top of a short pillar, she spared a look back. Ajax came running around the bend in the road, caught sight of her, and let out a few triumphal yips. Calix sat on the post a couple seconds more, trying to catch her breath. She was nearing the end of her stamina; she could feel it.

"Scratch, I may not be able to pull this off." she whispered into the night air, "I have to try."

She leapt from the column to a stone railing and ran, Ajax almost just beneath her, calling her name with every breath.

"Almost, almost," she repeated to herself.

This part was going be risky. She'd intended to be well in front of them at this point, but there was nothing she could do about that now. With a quick intake of breath to steal her courage she jumped down and landed running, right in front of Ajax.

He snapped his jaws and she felt hairs ripped from the tip of her tail, pulled free by his teeth. Calix ran for all she was worth, separating the distance between them in one spurt of effort as they rounded a bend in the terrace road they were on. She was ready to give up when a blessedly loud voice shouted "NOW!"

Behind her, there was a metallic snap of a catch being released. A gate, kept closed under the tension of a tightly wound spring, snapped open and slammed right into Ajax, who ran into it at full speed. The force of the collision sent Ajax reeling backward and, off balance and confused, he was not prepared for the gate to keep moving.

As Calix stopped and turned, she caught the slightest hint of his paws showing through from underneath the gate as it pushed him to the edge of the terrace and then launched him over the side. Ajax yelped in pain a few times, then became silent as his body crashed down the hill. In this part of Poros there were very few structures to break his fall.

For Calix, still trying to catch her breath, it was noise in the darkness.

Fluff's head popped up from where the latch to the gate was situated.

"I can't believe that worked!"

"You and me both Fluff, but I'm oh so glad it did, Ajax is the worst."

Fluff cocked his head a little.

"What about Elmax?"

"Oh crap!" Calix had momentarily forgotten about him.

Elmax had certainly not forgotten about them though. He came up the road and with a single heave brought both his paws up and pushed his weight on the gate. It swung back to its closed position and latched shut. He stopped to look at her, his tongue lolling out of one side of his mouth.

"Missed me."

"So you think!" Calix said, focusing her gaze behind him.

Elmax turned in alarm and Calix took off running, again.

She didn't have to run as fast or as far this time. Elmax didn't mindlessly sprint after anyone, he used his sense of smell and hunted.

He wasn't all that bright in a lot of ways, but in tracking he was very very good. Calix was counting on that, that and his arrogance. Still, she was exhausted from all the activity so far. She wanted to lay down and take a nap.

"Focus Calix," she said to herself.

She jumped out of her head and back into her surroundings, feeling a moment's panic as she didn't recognize anything around her, until the edge of a nearby rooftop brought everything into perspective, but where was Elmax?

He came from a different direction than behind her, almost got her too. She jumped to the side, hissed, then sprinted away again. This time in full flight mode. He'd played his trick, now he would be out for blood.

Sure enough, Elmax galloped up behind her. She put everything she had into running, catching sight of the bush, she broke for it hard, Elmax right on her tail. She crashed through the bush's branches and leaves, letting her body fall to the barren ground underneath as she struggled to catch her breath.

Something loomed over her in the darkness.

"What a fool you are Calix, did you really think a bush would stop me? You even brought me right to the new mother and her little ones by the smell of it. I'm sorely disappointed in you. I thought you and Nyke were more capable"

Calix lay there panting, too out of breath to respond.

Chapter Twenty-Three

Dahlia

DAHLIA SNIFFED AROUND A raised ledge just inside a cave she'd found during her exploration. It didn't smell as if any other creatures used this spot but it never hurt to double check. Especially if she was going to hide her kittens here should the need arise.

She'd found it by accident when she'd lost her footing on a rock and slipped and fallen. After she'd gotten herself sorted out, she'd noticed the entrance, angled slightly down the slope of the island and somewhat hidden from easier thoroughfares. Curious, she'd approached and found it to be the right size for her, but conveniently too tight a fit for a dog. Or rather, any dog small enough to fit through that hole, she could easily handle on her own.

Having come that far and not found much, she'd decided to examine this cave. A short way in there was a cross tunnel that branched off directly downslope. She'd had no desire to attempt climbing up or down and so she'd continued on with the tunnel she was in. A few tails deeper in it began to curve back upward.

She was about to turn back when she'd noticed this ledge. It was midway up the tunnel wall and had a small little cave of its own dug out of the earth behind it. Dahlia could barely contain her excitement.

It was the perfect size for a nursery and oh so much safer than hiding under a bush. And so here she was sniffing around, trying to ascertain if another cat or other living thing called this place home. It didn't appear as if they did so this place was free for the taking.

"Perhaps I should move them now?" she said to herself.

It was a tempting idea, but she didn't know what was going on outside. She imagined moving them right into the crossfire of Calix and Nyke's plan. That would not be good.

"No, if it looks like their plan will fail, that's when I will move them."

Dahlia hopped back over the cross tunnel and out the entrance she'd discovered. She spent a little time familiarizing herself with the location so she wouldn't lose it if she had to get here in a rush. After that she began making her way back to the bush. Pausing occasionally to leave scent markers for herself should she need them.

Halfway back, she stopped, sniffed the air.

The smell of grilled fish wormed its way up her nostrils and into her brain. Her stomach clenched, reminding her that her last meal was long gone.

Looking around, she began to follow the smell. It was close, very close.

Soon a huge green bin loomed up in front of her, covered with what looked to be a black lid. There was a little space between the lid and the bin, and it was from this space that the smell of grilled fish emanated.

Dahlia looked at it intently, trying to work out a way she could get through that lid.

"Hiya!"

Suddenly crouching with ears tucked tightly against her head Dahlia swiveled around trying to find who had spoken.

"Where are you?!" she hissed

"Um, up here, yoohoo!"

Dahlia's eyes climbed up the length of the bin. She almost jumped when they reached the top. Lying there, head leaning out over the side was a young black cat. Big green eyes and even bigger ears focused on her, but there was nothing but sincere curiosity on its face.

"I'm Verily! You here for the fish too? I bet we could get this lid off if we work together..."

"Not, as long as you're sitting on it, no?"

Verily blinked, looked around as if startled by something, then said, "Right!"

As she spoke, she jumped off the bin, and approached Dahlia to sit down right in front of her. She sat there, looking at Dahlia expectantly with those big eyes of hers. Dahlia was not quite sure what to do next.

"The lid?" she asked.

Verily cocked her head to the side "Lid? Oh! The lid! Yes! Yes! Yes! I have an id..."

Dahlia rolled her eyes and turned her attention to study the bin as Verily chased a moth that had suddenly flitted by.

"Either I figure this out, or it isn't happening" she said to herself.

"Godd it!" Verily shouted through a mouthful of moth.

Dahlia ignored her and began to walk around the bin wondering how that little youngster had gotten on top of it. She found that the bin had been placed sideways along a stone wall, its top almost aligned with the lip of the bin. Thanks to some rocks piled up she was able to jump up to the top of the wall and began looking hard at the place where the lid met the bin. She sniffed and probed with her paws, looking for a place where she might be able to squeeze one in. It was difficult, the lid seemed to be weighed down by something.

"What ya doin?"

Dahlia jumped and lost her purchase on the wall, digging her claws in and stopped herself for a moment. Just long enough to see Verily's blank and open expression watching with curiosity, from atop the lid. Then she lost her grip and slid down the side of the wall. She hit the ground with a little thump but was otherwise ok.

In short order she was back on the wall.

"Would you mind?" Dahlia said to Verily, who stared at her blankly for a moment, then realized Dahlia was gesturing.

Soon enough though, she understood what Dahlia was trying to do and added her own prying paws to the equation. Without Verily's weight on it, the lid proved much easier to move.

Both her and Verily were able to get paws underneath the lid, then their heads. Fortunately, the bin was full almost to the brim and the remains of several grilled fish were sitting right on top.

Dahlia and Verily began eating as fast as they could. Dahlia, driven by hunger and a need to get back to her kittens. Verily by, whatever it was that made adolescent cats need to constantly eat.

So it was that they were both tucked under the lid of the trash bin with their hindquarters sticking out when Lucky's warning yowl sounded across the island. Dahlia might not have noticed but for Verily, who jumped so violently she flipped the lid over on its hinges, opening the bin completely

"Oh no! Oh no! Oh no! I have to go! I'm sorry!"

"Wait, what? Why?"

Verily paused and motioned up the slope.

"The warning! The bad ones are loose! I have to go!"

"The warning?" Dahlia asked, but she was talking to herself. Verily was already gone.

Dahlia looked up the slope, her eyes widening as comprehension dawned on her.

"The warning!"

She was down off the bin in an instant. Racing off, she started to panic but then stomped on it, saying a little prayer to Bastet instead.

"Blessed mother keep them safe until my return, this is my one request."

She ran on, resolve solidifying in her mind. She prepared herself to attack anything that was threatening her young ones. She flexed her claws as she ran, loosening them and readying them for battle.

Still, relief flooded her as she rounded a corner to find the bush unmolested. She got the sense there were a lot of other cats around but couldn't see anything to confirm this. She put it out of her mind and ran into the bush.

There they were, curled up with each other, sleeping soundly, tiny ears or paws occasionally twitching. She approached them, purring loudly from her chest, waking them up, for surely, they were hungry by now.

They were just starting to stir when another cat raced into the bush and lay down panting. Dahlia turned but couldn't quite make out who it was or decide if she should be alarmed.

"Who is it?" she called out, testing.

She was just about to move closer to see who it was when a voice sounded out of the darkness.

"I've just c-c-come from above. It has b-b-begun." Nyke said through quick breaths.

A loud yelp and the sound of something crashing through brush in the distance punctuated his words.

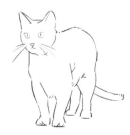

Chapter Twenty-Four

Calix

CALIX LAY ON THE ground, her chest heaving as she sucked air in attempts to catch her breath. A dark shape loomed over her in the shadows underneath the bush. She could just make out a pair of fangs revealed by curled back lips as a low growl began to vibrate the air around her.

Completely spent, her muscles in full rebellion, she could barely move her legs, much less stand up and move around. A few deep breaths and her breathing began to slow enough for her to speak. She looked up toward the shape looming over her and said...

"He's all yours. Remember the deal, no killing"

The growl deepened but otherwise Barnabus gave no reply as he pushed his way out from under the bush, head held low, to confront Elmax.

"Dammit Calix, move! You know you want to watch this!" she said to herself. Pushing herself, she was able to move herself into a position where she had a relatively wide field of view out from under the bush.

"I bet ol Barnabus was a shock for you." Calix thought to herself.

That did indeed look to be the case, Elmax's posture said everything about how unprepared he had been to find himself facing someone of equal if not greater stature. He lowered his head and watched as Barnabus stalked toward him, gauging him.

"Well. Well. Well. I guess they're cleverer than I gave them credit for. No matt..."

Barnabus charged.

Calix's tail flicked in amusement as Elmax almost rolled over on his back in a scramble to back up and not be caught unprepared.

He almost made it.

He'd underestimated Barnabus's desire for retribution. He was also not that accustomed to being so aggressively confronted. Calix glanced around, spotted Anthos sitting on a rooftop watching quietly.

Anthos, a joy to Barnabus and a reminder.

He'd promised Anthos's mother he'd help protect her and her kittens. She'd been on the move toward the mainland and gotten stuck giving birth in Poros. The council had asked Barnabus, whose human was a sort of an animal healer, if he would help look after them until her and her children were ready to move on. Barnabus had agreed.

What ended up happening was tragic beyond what anyone could have anticipated.

Elmax had found them, cornered the mother and her little ones in sight of Barnabus, but out of his reach. Barnabus had gotten the rope his human kept him tethered to tangled up on something.

He'd strained himself into unconsciousness trying to reach the mother and kittens as Elmax tauntingly savaged them right in front of him. Anthos had been the only one to survive, and that only because of the skills of Barnabus's human.

Calix's tail dropped with a thump. *"A very nasty business"* she thought.

Elmax had completely misjudged Barnabus's pain and ire, so he hadn't been expecting his charge to just keep coming. He'd almost found his feet again when Barnabus slammed into him, sending them both rolling.

As they slid to a halt Calix noticed that Barnabus had his jaws clamped firmly over Elmax's throat while the latter flailed his legs around trying to find purchase. Elmax's paws found a large rock and, bracing against it, he was able to twist himself out of Barnabus's grasp. He stood up and backed off, growling and snarling.

"Oh scratch, this could get ugly" Calix muttered.

Barnabus was larger than Elmax, but leaner, Elmax was smaller, but stockier. Elmax would have a much easier time getting to Barnabus's throat. Still Barnabas could use his greater size to try to force Elmax onto his back. To force a submission.

Calix wondered briefly if she should help, but decided she would only get in the way. Besides, if Barnabus ended up in real trouble Anthos would probably rush in like a crazed badger. She could take her cue from him.

She looked toward Anthos for a moment, then back to the fight.

Elmax had somehow gotten up over Barnabus's shoulders and clamped down on him just at the base of his neck. He kept raising up and pushing his weight against Barnabus in an attempt to force him to the ground on his side.

Barnabus was simply too big for this to work, Elmax couldn't bring his center of gravity up high enough to overbalance him.

"Always with the dominance play, eh Elmax?" Calix mused, shaking her head a little,"You're such a fool."

For his part, Barnabus was pushing back against Elmax's attempts to overpower him while also trying to look for a place he could bite down and get some leverage. Their positions were making that difficult for him though, and Calix could tell that the grip Elmax had on the back of his neck was putting him in a lot of pain.

"Well, never mind," Calix said, "you might actually have Barnabus at a disadvantage."

Anthos apparently thought so too. Glancing toward him, Calix noticed the other cat had stood up and looked poised to join the fight.

Then there was a loud SNAP!

" o o o w w o o o o w w w o w w w o w o o o o o o o o O o O o O o w - WOWOOOOOOOOOOOOOOOOOOOOOOOOO!"

The cry of pain was one of the most heart wrenching things Calix had ever heard in her life. She whipped her head around, expecting to see Barnabus in some sort of losing position, but that's not what greeted her.

"OH" she said.

Elmax looked to have gotten one of his front legs stuck in some sort of hole or crack in the ground. As they'd struggled Barnabus's full weight had pushed against it at such an angle the bone had snapped right in two. Elmax lay on the ground, curled in on himself whimpering, Barnabus standing over him with a feral look in his eyes.

"Oh scratch it!" Calix muttered, "he promised no killing!"

She prepared herself to rush out there and try to stop Barnabas from finishing off Elmax. It didn't look like she would make it. His head was already lowering towards Elmax's throat, his mouth opening.

"Barnabus."

Everyone froze, that was a human voice, and not just any voice. This voice belonged to the human who cared for Barnabus. The one who had saved Anthos. It was not a voice Barnabus could ignore.

He stopped his move toward Elmax's throat and sat back on his haunches, looking up at his human expectantly. She patted one of her paws against her leg and Barnabus dutifully stood up, walked to her side and sat down.

She said something to him and then walked toward Elmax, who tried to curl in on himself more, the bottom part of his leg lay on the ground at an unnatural angle to the rest of him. Kneeling next to Elmax she began whispering things to him in a hushed tone. Then, to Calix's amazement, she reached out and touched him. Allowed him to sniff her and then nuzzled her paw, her slender digits caressing him softly, soothingly.

She appeared to examine Elmax's leg, then got up and poked around in the bush for a minute or two. She returned to Elmax holding a long thin piece of wood, from around her waist she took something long and thin. All the while she spoke to Elmax in calm, even, and soothing tones. Calix even found herself being calmed by the human's whispering.

Still whispering, she crouched next to Elmax and did something with his leg that made him yelp, snarl, and then pass out. When she stood up again, Calix could see that the leg had been aligned and the stick had been tied to the leg to keep it in place.

The human looked around, then let out a deep sigh or resignation. She knelt down by Elmax and gently wormed her paws underneath his body. Then, slowly and gingerly, she picked him up, cradling him in her arms.

As she started walking away, she called Barnabus's name one last time and the big dog stood up and began trotting after her. He spared one last glance at Calix and nodded slightly, before turning and following his human home.

Calix sat in silence for a bit, pondering what might happen next with Elmax.

A strong, cool gust of wind ruffled her fur and brought her out of her reverie. Light rain drops pelted the ground around her.

"Guess, I should go check on Dahlia and Nyke."

Then she heard it, what sounded like the cries of hundreds of cats, raised in unison echoing across the island.

"Oh no" she breathed quietly, and wearily raced off, her worst fears playing out in her imagination.

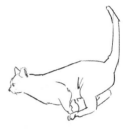

Chapter Twenty-Five

Ajax

Patt

His body lays motionless in the brush.

He sleeps. Or does he?

Images of snuggling up to his mother roll across his mind's eye, her large body filling his vision. The warm wiggling bodies of his siblings all around him, all of them driven by the same two needs, comfort and hunger.

Patt

He plays, he runs, he barks, he rolls. A bell rings, a voice calls out. He looks up, his sister's ear flopping out of his mouth as she also pauses to look. Food? Food! A mad rush. He runs so fast his back legs out pace his forelegs, and he nosedives into the ground in a summersault. Those behind him crash into him until they're nothing but a big ball of puppies, struggling to right themselves.

Pitt patt

He is put in a box, but he can see out of it. His siblings are with him, and they all make themselves dizzy watching a blur of landscape rush past them. One by one, they lay down to sleep, curling up together for warmth and comfort. He's the last to get tired and he burrows into the pile seeking warmth and comfort. He whimpers, they all do, softly talking to each other, reassuring each other.

Pitt

He's in another box, at least he thinks so. He can't see the box, but if he moves too far in any direction, he runs into something. He can rise up on his hind legs and brace his paws against it. There are many humans, they come and go. They whimper and yip at them, paw at them, wondering if they have food. Small humans come and knock on the box, they press their paws and faces against its invisible walls.

He tries to lick them.

Pitt patt patt

He is alone in the box. One by one his siblings disappeared. Taken by humans. Sometimes he would see them running outside the box, but he couldn't get to them. Occasionally he is taken out of the box and put in a small room with a human or humans. They play with him for a little while. Give him toys that he can bite and shake. He likes those times. He likes the toys. The box is boring by comparison.

Patt

He wonders if a human will come and take him. Then one day, one does. This human doesn't pet him though. It just stuffs him in another box and leaves him there for a long time. When the box is open again, he's in a different place. He tries to play with the human, like he played with the others.

Instead of petting him or giving him toys, the human yells and hits him and kicks him. He shies away but tries again and again. All his attempts bring only violence and anger. He begins to mimic the human. Begins to yell and snap at anything not the human. That gets him a few blessed pats on the head.

Patt pitt patt

He's found some toys! They are a little different, they are the same size and shape, but they are alive. They squeal and squirm as he plays with them. After a while, they stop, broken. His human finds him, gives him praise for the first time. He is ecstatic! He looks for more toys, but only sometimes finds them.

Patt patt

The human introduces Elmax. Elmax is so smart. Elmax teaches him new words. Like cat and kittens and birds, all toys to him, but nice to know they have names. He does too! Elmax named him. Ajax. He likes it. He tries to tell the human and gets a beating for his trouble. Elmax laughs at him, and he digs a hole to hide in for a while.

Patt

Elmax has found a way out of their big box! Together they look for toys. He loves toys! He lowers his nose to the ground, searching for their scent. His ears raise as he listens for their mews. Elmax beside him asks "do you smell them?"

CRRRRaackkk

The clap of the thunder snaps his eyes open. He is lying tangled in the brush. Confused, he does not remember where he is or how he got here. His body hurts in places, he can smell his own blood and, something else.

Sniff sniff

His ears pick up and he mouths a single word.

"Kittens!"

Ajax howls his excitement. Rain begins to fall, soaking into his fur, as he charges off, following the unmistakable scent of a mother and her kittens.

Time to play.

Chapter Twenty-Six

Dahlia

DAHLIA TURNED HER ATTENTION to the noise of something crashing through the brush down the steep hillside of Poros. Thinking back to the plan as it had been described to her, she cocks her head to listens a little longer then looks down at Nyke, who is still catching his breath.

"Ajax?"

He blinks an acknowledgement.

"Yes, if all went to p-p-plan. I rushed back here as s-s-soon as the alarm cry s-s-sounded"

Dahlia looked back toward where the sound had come from. She had her doubts about this part of the plan. As she'd been told, they'd intended to toss Ajax down the side of the island in an area where there wasn't much to break his fall. If he survived, he'd end up near the shoreline where many humans would be at this time of the evening. If he made it that far, he would almost certainly end up attacking one. Once he did that, the humans would take care of that problem. Technically the plan had three possible solutions with Ajax being either dead or too wounded to chase anything or being dealt with by humans.

It had sounded good when they told her, but the more she thought about it, the slimmer those possibilities seemed.

Nyke spoke, bringing her out of her reverie.

"There s-s-seems to be a great many c-c-cats gathered outside, did you n-n-notice?"

"I got that impression when running back after hearing the alarm, but didn't see any of them, more like I felt their presence."

Nyke's eyes widened... "You w-w-went out?"

"Yes, but only to..."

"Nyke? Dahlia? Nyke? Are you both in there?"

They both looked up at Mikos's shout.

"Is that Mikos?" Dahlia asked.

"Dahlia, I n-n-need to kn-kn-know where you..."

Dahlia wasn't listening, she'd already started outside to see why Mikos was calling for them.

She exited the bush to find Mikos sitting there with two other cats. All around them, the trees, rocks, fences and rooftops bristled with the silhouetted ears of cats.

Dahlia's breath caught.

"So many," she thought to herself. She would never have guessed that this many cats lived on Poros.

"Ah Dahlia, good to see you again, is Nyke in there also?"

She turned her head back toward the entrance and was about to respond when Nyke exited, coming to sit next to her.

"M-M-Mikos," he said acknowledging the cat, then more cooly "Ph-ph-phira, Hera."

Both looked away, as if in shame, something Dahlia thought odd. Nyke continued though.

"I c-c-cannot stay to talk, there is s-s-something I must check on, and it c-c-cannot wait."

He then hurried off without a second thought for either of them. As he disappeared out of view the sounds of two dogs battling one another echoed down the slope of the island.

"Well, that's one part going as planned" Dahlia thought. She turned her attention back to Mikos.

"Why are you here?" she asked, "Why are all of you here?' Her eyes roaming around to indicate she meant all the cats hanging about.

"Well, this is my idea. To help you" Mikos said. "Coincidentally, our meeting gave me inspiration for it."

Dahlia thought back to earlier in the day, she couldn't think of anything that would make him think bringing every cat here would help her. Then she remembered being kicked off the side of the quay and Calix jumping in with her. Nyke and Mikos had made such a racket that a kindly human had come and fished them out of the water.

"You intended to make such a noise that the humans would be unable to ignore it, thus enlisting their aid?"

Mikos stood up in excitement... "Yes! Yes! That's precisely it! I went to the council and convinced them to gather everyone to come to your aid with exactly that plan."

He nodded toward the other two with him.

"This is Hera and Phira, two of the current longest sitting members of the council"

They blinked their acknowledgement. Then the one Mikos had named Hera spoke.

"Once this is over, we shall help you find a safe space to raise your kittens. Though if all goes according to plan, the greatest danger to them will be gone"

Dahlia understood immediately why Calix did not like Hera, she was one of those cats who added a patronizing tone to virtually everything she said. Dahlia found herself wanting to argue with her, just because. Instead, she looked back to Mikos.

"Well Mikos, it appears as if we won't need to use your plan."

As Mikos opened his mouth to reply two things happened.

A light rain started up and a gust of wind blew through the area, seeming to carry with it the howl of a dog in a great deal of pain, but also, excitement?

"That can't be right," Dahlia said.

"You heard it as well?" the one named Phira asked.

Mikos's head was cocked, "It sounded as if that howl came from two separate locations."

"It sounded like both Ajax and Elmax, is what," Hera said.

They sat listening, trying to hear more, but the wind and light patter rain were making it difficult. Dahlia began to feel uneasy; she got up to go back and check on her kittens. That's when a warning yowl rose from a little further down the terrace they were on.

"Wha..." Mikos said.

"Oh scratch" Hera said, "It's Ajax!"

His approach could be seen in a wave of arched backs and hisses from the watching cats. Fast and relentless, he moved with a speed that shocked Dahlia. As Ajax came into view, charging straight toward them, he barked a single word over and over with every stride.

"Kittens! Kittens! Kittens! Kittens!"

Hera and Phira scattered. Dahlia found herself trapped by fear, he was running right towards her, eyes locked on hers, and she could do nothing.

"Move dammit! MOVE!" Her own mind screeched at her, but her muscles wouldn't respond.

He was almost upon her. She could feel her death in those jaws and was powerless to do anything to stop it. Then Mikos was there, in front of her. He'd turned himself sideways, arched his back and puffed out all of his fur. He looked larger than life, he was absolutely glorious. Dahlia found her muscles relaxing.

"HOW DARE YOU CO..." he began to hiss at Ajax.

Before he could finish Ajax reached him and chomped down on his throat. Dahlia watched in horror as Ajax began shaking his head back and forth. Miko's eyes were wide with fear as he scrambled to free himself from Ajax's jaws, his body flailing about as Ajax's head jerked.

One.

Two.

Three jerks.

There was an audible snap.

Mikos went limp in his grasp and, tossing the now lifeless body to the ground Ajax looked up, locking his gaze with hers.

Dahlia began to back away. Horror and fear had drained her of the ability to do anything. She wanted to cry out for Mikos, wanted to rush to her kittens, wanted to fight and run at the same time, it was all too much.

Ajax began to move toward her, his mouth opening, ready to take her like he'd taken Mikos. As he was about to snap at her though, something changed. He paused, and his eyes rolled as he let out a yelp of extreme pain. He turned and tried to nip at something behind him.

That's when Dahlia saw Nyke, Ajax's balls firmly gripped between his paws and his jaws clamped down on one of them as if he intended to eat it right off Ajax's body. The reprieve snapped Dahlia out of her paralysis, and she fled into the bush to her kittens, one thought on her mind.

"I've got to get them the scratch away from here!"

Chapter Twenty-Seven

Nyke

DAHLIA FLEEING BARELY REGISTERED to Nyke. Yes, he'd done what he did to save her, but he had his own issues at the moment.

Inside he was reeling from the loss of Mikos. His brash action had been to save him as much as Dahlia, but he hadn't been quick enough, and Nyke was struggling to keep down the wave of emotion his failure had set loose in him. If only he hadn't raced off to try and find where Dahlia had sprinkled her scent around their hiding place.

"Also, I've got a mouth full of scratching Ajax balls" he thought to himself.

What was worse, was the one he had clamped down on had sort of disintegrated in his jaws so he'd switched to the other, and now one of his fangs was stuck in it. Trying to work his fang loose while avoiding Ajax's attempts to get at him was difficult enough, but Ajax's tail kept trying to curl down between his legs and ended up blinding him instead. It was only a matter of time before Ajax caught him with a nip, then it would be over.

"Calix will never let it go if I die with Ajax's balls in my mouth."

The thought came as Ajax tried backing up quickly. Nyke found himself on his back, Ajax's body hovering above him.

Without a thought his claws extended, his hind legs went to work raking the length of Ajax's underside faster and faster. Deep scratches appeared along Ajax's belly and Nyke could hear him yelping in pain once again.

"Good" Nyke thought with a sense of pleasure.

Ajax moved forward again to get away from Nyke's claws. Nyke, whose fang was still frustratingly stuck in Ajax's scrotum, had to curl his body up as his head was pulled forward. Rolling his body in a summersault, Nyke found himself in the same position as a moment before. Standing upright right behind Ajax, mouth full of balls, or ball as it were.

Ajax went back to trying to fold himself in half to get a nip at Nyke and pull him free. Things were not looking good. His fang was still stuck and nothing he could do seemed capable of pulling it loose.

A sudden sharp pain traveled up his spine and blossomed in his mind. Ajax had gotten a hold of his tail.

Nyke tried to prepare himself for the pain of having at least part of his tail torn from his body. He'd seen it happen to others, and it had sort of looked like an instant pain and then get on with your life kind of thing.

Before Ajax could yank his tail off though a blur flew out of the shadows and slammed bodily into him. Ajax released Nyke's tail as he was thrown on his side. He howled again as Nyke's fang was finally torn free of his sensitive bits by the force of the movement.

Nyke's view expanded as he scrambled backward away from Ajax's back end. The blur resolved itself into Calix, fur puffed and back arched as she danced around on the tips of her paws hissing obscenities. Nyke, righting himself, had never been so happy to see his friend in his life.

"M-M-My thanks." he managed to say.

"Pfff," Calix sniffed. "If you think I was going to let you meet your end with a mouth full of Ajax's balls, I don't know that we can remain friends."

Nyke opened his mouth to reply but noticed that Ajax had recovered from the body slam and, despite his injuries, seemed to be deciding which of them to attack first. He seemed just about to move when another body slammed into him from the other side.

Nyke looked toward their new ally, trying to see who it was.

"Ph-Ph-Phira?" he said aloud.

The dainty council member stood before Ajax. Ears thrust forward; she looked like she was about to challenge Ajax to a fight to the death. She darted forward as Ajax turned and hit his face with rapid fire blows from her paws, aiming for his eyes. Ajax seemed taken aback for a second, but then gathered himself to snap at her throat and do to her what he'd done to Mikos. He never got there though.

As Nyke watched, Phira backed up and let out a wail so deep and so loud he guessed it could be heard across the entire island. Ajax cocked his head to the side to listen for a moment, then began to move again, but stopped short.

Another voice added itself to Phira's as Hera slowly walked out of the shadows to stand next to her.

Then another,

and another,

and another.

Nyke was surprised to hear his own voice added to the song as hundreds of cats voiced their pain, their fear, their lament and their lives. Together, the cats of Poros yowled their defiance at the tyranny over their lives that Elmax and Ajax held. It was Miko's plan, coming to fruition and a dirge for his passing all at once.

Nyke was overwhelmed.

So too, was Ajax.

He half lay down. His eyes wide as he took in all the cats around him, meowing their loudest, their deepest, their most heartfelt songs. Every single one of them focused on him.

For the first time since Nyke had known of him, Ajax seemed to be aware that others existed. Not as prey, or playthings, but as others. He sat there, bleeding from many different wounds, looking like nothing so much as a puppy, lost and alone. Nyke shook his head, he had no intention of feeling empathy for this killer. This dog who had taken so many of those he'd known, so many that he'd called friends.

He looked at Calix, and his world twisted and changed again.

Calix sat there, infuriatingly relaxed as if no danger existed, looking at Ajax with nothing but pity in her eyes. She looked up and made eye contact with Nyke, and he saw it, nothing but sorrow for Ajax.

"What the hell!?" he thought.

Before he was able to confront Calix though, a human entered the scene. Drawn by the noise of hundreds of cats yowling into the night simultaneously.

She came wielding a broom, which she used to clear cats from the nearby walls and fences. A look of shock crossed her face as she came across Ajax, surrounded by Nyke, Calix, Hera and Phira. Ajax shrunk in on himself while the others scattered into the shadows.

Nyke watched as the human knelt beside Ajax. An expression of recognition crossed her face, she pulled something out of her pocket. After making noises into it for a few minutes she slipped it back into her pocket. The human reached out an exploratory paw towards Ajax, who was laying on his side now. He allowed her to touch his head, closing his eyes as he did so.

Presently, Barnabus's human came into view.

After a brief conversation with the first human, she scooped up Ajax and carried him away. The first human soon followed.

"What the hell? Why do they suddenly care so much about those dogs? It's not like they'd spared a whisker before." Calix said. Her words echoed into the silence left behind by the human's passing.

"I'm j-j-just glad it's over." Nyke said, walking over to Calix his tail shot up into the air as he brushed his head against Calix's chin.

"I hope it was all worth it." Calix replied.

A flash of lightning ripped through the sky, making them all shrink back.

As thunder rumbled behind it, the clouds opened up and the trickle of rain that had come with Ajax's entrance became a thick downfall with sheets of water pouring down from the sky.

They all headed for the bush, set as it was, it would remain relatively dry inside.

Once inside Calix visibly looking around said.

"Where's Dahlia?"

Nyke found himself looking around also, a flash of lightning lit up the entire area.

"M-m-more importantly," he replied, "Where are her k-k-kittens?"

Chapter Twenty-Eight

Verily

THE EVENING HADN'T BEEN going too well for Verily.

She'd spent a fair portion of the day trying to figure out how to get to some fish and when she finally got to them, the alarm had sounded. She'd rushed off to her usual hiding spot only to find it occupied by a mean old male whose name she couldn't remember.

"Scram!" he'd said in his scratchy old voice, showing off his fangs with a hiss.

"Well, one fang. He was missing one" she thought. Then she giggled to herself remembering all the names she'd come up for him as she'd run away and listing them in her mind.

"Fangy, Sir One Fang, Monofang, Fangboy, Mr. Fang of the Halffangs.."

She chittered to herself in amusement as she looked around, watching the area from her current hiding spot atop a narrow stairway tucked between two clay pots. It was starting to rain and judging from the sky, it would be getting worse. She tried to listen for the alarms, the warning cries that would give away the positions of those two dogs that liked to get loose and run around hurting cats.

Verily shuddered, her ears folding in close to her head.

"I DO NOT want to run into them."

She'd come across Elmax once by straying too close to their yard. He'd tried to coax her closer to him with kind sounding words and entreaties. He'd gone so far as to promise her a ride on his back, which almost got her.

"I mean, how fun would that be?!" she asked herself. She once again spared a moment, letting her imagination run wild with the thought of clinging to some huge dog's back as it ran at top speed through the narrow lanes of Poros. She decided she'd ask Barnabus if he'd be game for it, assuming she could get past Anthos.

"He IS very protective of his dog" she thought.

That's when something caught her eye. Motion in the shadows, but fast. She turned her attention to it, but after a few seconds nothing happened. Chalking it up to her imagination, Verily went back to what she'd been thinking about.

"Wait, what was I thinking about?"

Another flash of movement caught her eye. Her paws pumped up and down in excitement.

"That was definitely not my imagination!"

She waited, eyes wide open, ears pointed forward, all zeroed in on the spot where she'd seen movement. No more thoughts entered her mind, not a single thing existed but that one spot, she wanted to be ready.

Motion

Verily leapt from the stairs, lightly touched the top of a barrel using the brief contact to maintain her momentum. She hit the ground in full sprint, making a straight line for the spot where she'd seen movement. Slowing as she drew nearer, she crouched down and began to crawl forward, step by step. Coming to rest behind a rock, she flattened her body out in its shadow, waiting, all of her attention filtering through her eyes and ears.

She heard it first, the soft pads of something running. Her hind legs began to pump up and down, her tail straightened out ready for the leap.

Motion

Verily's body leapt into the ambush before she even knew what was happening. Her awareness caught up to her and a vision of the cat she'd met earlier, growing larger and larger as she closed the distance, swam into her awareness.

There was a kitten unceremoniously dangling from her mouth looking a little nonplussed by the ordeal.

It yawned.

Verily pulled herself up, raising up on her hind legs in an attempt to slow her momentum and keep herself from crashing into... 'Dahlia!' she remembered. Her tail whipped to the side as a counterweight and she changed her trajectory, half jumping over and half past Dahlia, who just stood there watching, wide eyed.

Once she'd stopped and gotten herself sorted Verily turned to Dahlia.

"I'm sorry I'm sorry I'm sorry, I thought you would be food!" she said.

Dahlia looked at her warily but said nothing.

"Duh," Verily thought, *"she has a kitten in her mouth."*

The kitten licked its lips and began to squirm around. The movement seemed to break Dahlia out of whatever thought processes she'd been trapped in. Without any indication that Verily was there, she turned and dashed off into the darkness.

"Hey wait!"

Verily rushed after her, finding it difficult to keep up, she set such a fast pace. Quickly though, Verily found herself pulling up short as she saw Dahlia enter a round cave opening, and not come out.

She looked up and then around, rain was starting to fall in earnest now.

"Oh no oh no oh no, this is not good, this is NOT good" she said aloud. She went after Dahlia, down into the darkness of the cave, she came to the cross tunnel and made to cross. A paw smacked her across the nose. Reeling back Verily could just make out Dahlia blocking her path.

"Stay Away!" Dahlia hissed at her, "I will hurt you if you come any closer!"

"You don't understand! It's not safe in ..."

"It's not safe out there!" Dahlia screeched at her, "Mikos is already dead!" She seemed to deflate upon herself "It was so fast, so fast."

"Mikos?" asked Verily, "How..."

"They're all there too! Nyke, Hera... So many, it's not safe, not safe"

Dahlia lapsed into mumbling. Verily was at a loss, she had no idea what to do. She wasn't even sure if Dahlia was talking to her or herself. Soft mews from behind Dahlia caught her attention.

"Are those your kittens?"

Dahlia's eyes snapped to focus on her.

"He can't have them. He WON'T have them!" she said.

"Ok ok, but Dahlia, the rain..."

"Leave us alone! Verily? Verily. Leave us alone, we are safe here!"

"That's just it, you're no..."

"We are safe from HIM here! That is all that matters, come no closer Verily. I do not want to have to hurt you."

"Ok ok. I'll not bother you."

Verily was in no mood for a fight so she turned and left the cave. She had no idea what to do. Dahlia was in great danger though, if it rained hard enough, that cave would fill up with rushing water. Dahlia and her kittens would drown and be flushed out to sea all at once. Verily knew from experience, she'd lost a sibling to the dangers of that tunnel.

A noise that sounded very much like hundreds of cats crying out in unison caught her attention. Remembering what Dahlia had said about Nyke and Hera, that they were all together, she decided to head in that direction.

"Maybe one of them can help me convince her." she said.

The voices died down but Verily knew the spot, everyone did. Calix and Nyke were pretty popular. As she made her way there, she had to briefly duck into some cover as a human walked past in the night.

"That was Barnabus's human." she realized.

The sight of Barnabus's human set her mind back to imagining herself, sitting atop Barnabus as he ran and ran and ran. Wind on her face as she closed her eyes and pretended she was flying. She was so engrossed in this that she didn't even register Barnabus's human walking back, Ajax in her arms.

Then the sense of cats all around her snapped her attention out of her imagination. She looked around at the scene. Not much to indicate anything had happened, save for a hundred or so cats all gathered together. Her eyes fell upon Mikos's body.

"Ohhh" Verily quietly mouthed to herself.

A flash of lightning illuminated the area and she saw Nyke, Calix and a few others disappear into the bush they used as refuge. Verily moved to follow as heavy rain began to pour down. She got to the entrance just as another cat, Phira, was coming back out. Verily bowed her head in respect but Phira moved past without acknowledging her. Verily watched as she moved toward Mikos's body and lay down next to him, letting the rain soak her fur. Another flash lit the scene, Phira looked as if she was huddling Mikos for warmth.

Not knowing what to make of that, Verily entered the interior of the bush just in time to hear Nyke say.

"M-m-more importantly, where are her k-k-kittens?"

Nyke, Calix and Hera all looked startled as Verily abruptly interrupted their conversation.

"OO OO! I know where they are, I know where they are!"

Calix took a step toward her.

"Where?" she asked.

"The water tunnels." Verily said more quietly.

Hera and Nyke groaned as Calix cursed.

"Oh scratch it all! What is she thinking?"

Even as she complained, Calix was moving to leave, Nyke right behind her. She paused and looked up to Verily.

"You coming?"

"Wher... Oh, yes. Yes. Follow me." Verily said, and with that, she led them toward the entrance to the water tunnels where she'd confronted Dahlia.

Chapter Twenty-Nine

Dahlia

DAHLIA LOOKED TOWARD HER little ones as they nursed. Their small bodies looked like nothing so much as fuzzy, shifting shadows in the low light of the tunnel.

"Finally, we are safe," she said.

The air around them vibrated as a purr rumbled to life deep in her chest, joining the chorus of her kittens as their purrs reverberated within the confined of their new safe haven.

Dahlia lay her head down and focused on the pin pricks of pain created by their tiny claws kneading her as they suckled. Her purring sputtered in fits and starts as she struggled to keep the vision of Miko's last few seconds of life from playing through her mind over and over.

"No." she said to herself, pushing back as panic tried to assert itself again.

"We. Are. Safe."

Verily's words tried to intrude into her thoughts. She pushed back on them too. The tunnel was only a couple whiskers wide, there was no room for that dog, that monster, to fit.

One of the little ones moved away from feeding and began to squirm its way up toward her chin. Dahlia picked her head up, gave it a couple of sniffs and began grooming its little face with long slow passes of her tongue. The act strengthened her purr to a more consistent rumble, and she found her body relaxing into the motion.

Her kitten mewed.

Safe.

"Dahlia?"

Her mind went cold. Calix's voice was gentle, conciliatory, entreating. She wanted none of it. Swiveling her head, she could make out Calix's silhouette in the tunnel.

"Stay away from us Calix." she said calmly.

Then she laid her ears back and hissed at her.

"You're the worst Dahlia, but I'm not leaving. I won't come any closer, but there is something you need to know about these tunnels and I'm not going anywhere until you learn what that is. For the record though, we don't have a lot of time. Unless you're planning on having both you and your kittens swept out to sea that is. Would you mind if I came all the way over?"

Dahlia said nothing, she was suddenly focused on the little stream of water flowing beneath the arch of Calix's body. The sound of it filling in the details of what she couldn't quite see.

"Is there more water flowing than before?" she thought to herself. Then she noticed the amount water flowing along the bottom of the tunnel she was in had indeed increased.

She glanced up again.

Calix's face was so close their whiskers touched.

"Oh sc...!"

Dahlia rolled into a standing position sending her kittens somersaulting toward the back of the ledge. Her arched back pushed against the top of the cave, she tried to back up but there was no room. Calix's paw lashed out and began batting her right between the eyes as Calix herself began chanting out a lecture. Punctuating her words with whacks to Dahlia's face.

"Listen here you stubborn, spoiled, belly scratching kit."

whack

"These are HUMAN made caves."

whack

"When it rains, as it is now, they drain all the water..."

whack

"...from higher up on the island..."

whack

"...down to the sea!"

whack

Calix stopped swatting at her and looked her right in the eyes.

"We have minutes only Dahlia. Minutes! There is no time for debate, if you want you and your kittens to live, we have to get you and them out of here, and I mean right scratching now! If you even think of starting in with that Bastet business, I'll scratch your eyes out and save your kittens myself!"

Dahlia felt her anger rising to meet Calix's

"You can scratch off with your superior attitude Calix! We're safe here! You want to put me and my kittens in danger to suit YOUR plans and I am done! I'm not putting my kittens into the mouth of that beast! You can all go eat snails for all I care, and if you slander Bastet's name one more scratching time, I'll show you how I learned to fight! You're as awful as a magpie Calix, I shouldn't have trusted you."

Calix stood there silently for a long moment, then surprised her by saying.

"You're right, I'm sorry."

Dahlia watched as Calix deflated in front of her.

"You're right," she said again. "It was not right to use you and your little ones in that way. When the situation presented itself, I thought we had no choice but to act. I forgot that there is always a choice, even if it isn't very good."

She didn't know how to respond to that, so she just stared.

"Would you trust Verily? That kit doesn't have a malicious whisker on her face."

Dahlia was taken aback, wondering why Calix would bring up Verily, then...

"How does she know I met Verily?" she asked herself.

"She's the one who came and got us and showed us where you had hidden."

"Us?" Dahlia said, but she was still thinking of Verily.

That young cat couldn't hide her reactions to anything, and she'd followed Dahlia in here, tried to tell her. Dahlia's memory replayed the scene in her mind, letting her look at it with eyes and ears not blinded by panic.

"Verily lost a sibling to this very tunnel, swept away by flowing water, never to be seen again. She saw it happen and was powerless to do anything about it, they were only a few weeks older than yours when it happened."

The memory continued playing for Dahlia as Calix's words kept her mind focused on Verily.

"You don't understand! It's not safe..." Verily had said, and later *"The rain."*

The words came together in Dahlia's mind, combined with the very real fear for her Dahlia had heard in Verily's voice. Somehow, it pushed through the fog created by all the trauma of the day.

"Great Bastet what have I done? It's not safe here!" Dahlia cried.

"Finally!" Calix shouted with a sigh of relief. "Now let's get ou…"

She stopped mid-sentence, her ears swiveling as a new sound came echoing down the tunnel, from where it curved upward. A dull roar was moving its way down the tunnel toward the cross tunnel, and some sort of thumping noise. The cross tunnel itself was filling up with faster flowing water as more and more drained from uphill. Dahlia and Calix though only had ears for the noise, it almost sounded like purring, except for the thumping.

"Oh balls and claws there's the water!" Calix shouted.

Even as she'd said it the closeness of it became apparent and in the little bit of light that made it in through the tunnel entrance, they could just make out a gray shifting wall speeding toward them. Dahlia watched it come, realizing there was no time to save themselves or her kittens.

"Scratch it all." she heard Calix say bitterly.

THUMP

The sound snapped Dahlia's attention back up the tunnel. The roar had ceased, to be replaced by the trickling sound of water leaking through several smaller holes. A large branch had gotten lodged lengthwise against the sides of the tunnel, all the leaves and detritus that had been flowing at the head of the deluge had gotten stuck and more or less blocked the tunnel.

"Yeah ok, I should pray to Bastet more often." Calix said.

"Even now, she's got jokes" Dahlia thought, her tail flicking in irritation.

The wood blocking the tunnel groaned.

"Come on you poop eaters!"

Verily squeezed past Calix, edged up onto the ledge with Dahlia.

Dahlia started to react but Verily completely ignored her, mumbling a "Not this time" to herself.

Without glancing at Dahlia or Calix, she snatched up one of the kittens and raced back toward the tunnel entrance, having to force her way through a current of rushing water from the cross tunnel.

The action snapped Calix and Dahlia back to reality, as the branch holding back the tide from their tunnel groaned again under the weight of water. It slipped a little against the edges of the tunnel.

"Right!" Calix said, hopped up on the ledge, picked up a kitten, and followed Verily. Dahlia moved to follow, looking down at the two that were left. Both were mewing for her.

"I will be right back for you" she said to one, as she snatched up the other in her jaws, turned about and rushed away. She pushed through the cross tunnel. Icey water rushed around her body, and she almost released her jaws to scream from the shock of it. Her kitten mewed louder as the current almost made her lose her footing. Digging her claws into the other side of the cross tunnel she pulled her way forward, maintaining her grip on the lip of the other side of her tunnel.

Then she was through and out the tunnel entrance into the rain. Calix, Nyke, Hera, Verily and the kittens were all waiting.

"We n-n-need to get out of the r-r-rain!" Nyke said loudly.

Dahlia set the kitten in her mouth down with the others. "There's one left in the tunnel!" she said in a panic.

"I'll get it!" shouted Verily, turning toward the tunnel entrance.

"No." Calix said forcefully and aimed a blow at Verily that sent her tumbling back.

Before anyone could react, she rushed to the tunnel entrance and disappeared inside. Dahlia raced after her. As she entered the tunnel she watched as Calix's tail snaked its way through rushing water. Difficult as it was, she decided to wait, she had no way of knowing if she'd get in the way trying to cross.

The rushing current was really strong now. Time stretched out as agonizing moments of inaction stacked up on her back. Fear took over and she decided to cross and save her last kitten herself. As she moved forward though, Calix's face swam into view, an all-black kitten dangling from her mouth.

It was clear she was struggling with the current and holding on to the kitten. Dahlia moved forward to help if she could. Calix, for her part, pulled her body forward and dropped the kitten on the tunnel floor, this section had much less water. Dahlia snatched up her little one quickly and looked up. Her eyes widened as realization hit her.

The current of water from the cross tunnel was too strong. Calix had pushed off the lip of the other side of their tunnel with her hind legs. It had been just barely enough to be able to drop the kitten on the other side. The cost was that her hind legs had gotten caught in the current and swept down the tunnel.

Calix was clinging to this side with all her strength, claws digging in as deeply as they would go, but she was slipping.

With a kitten in her mouth, Dahlia couldn't do or say anything.

Calix looked up at her calmly and shouted "Go!"

Dahlia looked away indicating that she wasn't going to leave.

Calix's expression changed to one of resignation coupled with determination.

"Dahlia," she shouted, "It's ok, just go. Tell Nyke for me, kefi!"

With that last word Calix retracted her claws and vanished beneath the foam as the current dragged her down the cross tunnel toward the sea.

Before Dahlia could do anything further the log blocking the other tunnel split with a loud crack and a torrent of water and detritus could be heard rushing toward her.

Wracked with shame, Dahlia fled back through the entrance of the tunnel and out into the rain with her remaining kitten clasped firmly in her jaws.

Chapter Thirty

Nyke

NYKE SAT IN THE shade watching waves sweep in from the horizon to lap gently against the shore.

He watched, and waited, his mind replaying that night over and over again. The terror of fighting Ajax, the rush to find Dahlia, standing helpless in the rain as Dahlia exited the water tunnels alone with her last kitten. He'd looked past her, hoping, expecting, and then Dahlia had said those horrible words.

"I'm so sorry Nyke, she told me to tell you, kefi." The pain in her voice had made the rest obvious.

Kefi.

Nyke's stomach twisted at the farewell Calix left for him.

"Every moment of it Calix, every s-s-scratching moment."

He looked around, seeing this beach as it had been, the day they'd met.

He had come down to scrounge and scavenge away from the main quay. As often happens he got distracted by light waves, the sparkle of light reflecting off the water's surface. He loved losing himself in the endless dance of blues and whites, letting his mind wander.

Motion in the corner of his eye had caught his attention, and he'd turned just in time to see her. An emaciated youngster crouched behind a piece of driftwood. Her ears had been angled back and her eyes were wide and focused on him. As he'd turned, she'd pumped her hind legs a couple of times and then leapt toward him.

Nyke's tail twitched as the memory played itself out in his vision.

She'd tackled him before he could react, then jumped up and backed off. She hopped and crouched as if daring him to retaliate. It had taken only a moment for him to realize she'd wanted to play. He'd obliged her.

Looking down the beach he remembered seeing her running and jumping about. Rushing up to him only to skip away again playfully. What fun it had been, their first meeting.

"It's been over a full cycle of the moon Nyke,"

Visions of a young Calix faded and coalesced into Hera, walking toward him at an even pace.

"If she survived, she would have shown herself by now, don't you think?"

"P-p-perhaps, but I will never s-s-stop coming here to watch and wait."

"Suit yourself of course" Hera said as she took a seat next to him facing the water. "We've had news from Barnabus through Anthos."

"Oh?"

"Barnabus's human took Elmax to the mainland and came back without him. Lucky also reported seeing her confront Ajax and Elmax's human, it was quite loud, the way Lucky describes it. It may be that Elmax will never return."

"We c-c-can only hope."

"Ajax on the other hand, is with a different human. Living in their small little garden area. He had this great weird contraption on his head that kept him from cleaning himself. Looked awful, but it's gone now. He seems mostly healed but he just lays there under a tree, without doing much of anything."

"Perhaps the fight changed s-s-something in him?" Nyke mused aloud. Flashes of memory from that night threatened to overpower him. The urge to run and hide was strong.

"Who knows?" Hera replied. "Several have made themselves visible to him. He just glances at them and then looks away. Time will tell. Though we can't be too cautious where that one is concerned."

Nyke suppressed a sigh. He was finding it difficult to care about the goings on surrounding Elmax and Ajax, and the other reason Hera was here.

"Have you considered that other thing we talked about?" she asked.

Nyke did sigh this time.

"I'm s-s-sorry Hera, I do not think I want to run for Miko's s-s-seat on the council."

"But we NEED you Nyke. We need minds like yours. I can't take no for an answer."

"Ask me t-t-tomorrow."

"Very well." Hera said, "tomorrow then." She got up and left, having said what she wanted to say.

Nyke returned to his contemplation of water, lost again in his memories of Calix.

He'd taken her under his wing. Started showing her the ropes and explaining the rules. After playing on the beach, she'd told him how she'd come to be there. It was a story Nyke had heard many versions of. Her human had died. Some other humans had shown up and started taking all the things her human had had in their home. One of them had grabbed Calix and put her in one of those loud contraptions they zoomed around in. After a short time in there, they'd stopped, opened a door, and tossed her out into a bush. By the time she'd gotten herself freed from the bush, the humans were gone. They'd left her alone, in an unfamiliar place, devoid of humans.

She'd been alone for 3 days before making her way to this beach and seeing Nyke.

He thought about how he'd taught her about Poros and the council, of the rotation they'd set up for the quay and other places to get food from the humans. Taught her of the families, how they'd evolved into the council, and of the ones that were estranged from the main groups. Calix had been quick to grasp the politics of it all, and just as quick to reject it.

He remembered her first meeting Hera fondly.

"Who the scratch are you?!" she'd asked when Hera had caught her on the quay out of rotation and challenged her on it. Hera had sputtered in indignation.

Nyke's tail flicked back and forth in a silent laugh at the memory of Calix immediately mimicking Hera's sputtering.

"Ptpshjpshspg? That's a difficult name. Why did you choose it?"

Hera had only been able to sputter more.

Nyke lay down in the sand, stretching his body out, feeling the warmth and grittiness of it.

He'd been living on the fringes until she came along. Not taken seriously because of his tendency to stutter. No "family" had wanted to take him in, and even though the council ensured he got access to the food the humans doled out, he was still isolated.

Calix hadn't stood for that though. As social as he was reclusive, that one. She'd forged connections with other cats outside the boundaries of council mandates. She'd offered to be his voice to others. Had wanted to work together to help those the council ignored. Teaming up, they'd slowly helped reshape the territories of Poros, despite the council's attempts to keep things exactly as they were. They'd done it all outside the council's jurisdiction, probably one of the reasons Hera and Phira had viewed them as a threat.

Nyke stared at the water and tried to imagine how his life would be if he hadn't met Calix.

"Infinitely less interesting," he thought to himself.

Kefi.

She'd brought so much of that to his life, taught him to live with intention regardless of what the world threw at him. No, despite what the world threw at him.

Even in the most terrifying moment of his life, he'd found himself thinking of the inevitable joke Calix would make of the situation. She'd not disappointed him either, he recalled fondly.

He huffed, rested his chin on his paws.

"Please come back Calix," he thought out to the universe as sorrow surged up from the well of his heart, *"I do not know that I can do this without you."*

His vision went dark, and he felt as if he would be consumed by the pain. He floated there, inside his own mind, wanting to feel nothing, wanting to know nothing, wanting to be nothing.

As he sank further into the abyss of his loss, pin pricks of light began to intrude upon his consciousness. He tried to ignore them, but they demanded his attention. Blossoming for a second then receding, only to move and puncture his psyche again. He floated up out of the hole of his sorrow and realized the pricks of light represented actual physical pain.

Pain signals coming from the very tip of his tail.

Another flash of light, more insistent.

Nyke opened his eyes and rolled to the side to get a look at his tail, while simultaneously moving the whipping the tail away from whatever was causing the pain. He glanced and noticed a black kitten, laying in the sand behind him, paws out outstretched, eyes trying to focus on the tip of his swishing tail. Nyke looked further along the beach and saw Dahlia with three of her kittens wandering about, looking for a snack.

"S-s-so you're one of Dahlia's." He said as he stood up to face his attacker.

The kitten lay on its back, looking up at him as if just now realizing its "prey" was attached to something much larger. He lowered his head to sniff at it as it lay there staring up at him in amazement.

"You talk funny," it finally said, "why?"

"This is j-j-just how I t-t-talk."

"Oh,ok." it stretched out its paws, trying to swipe at his face, "wanna play?"

Nyke pretended to think about this for a moment then said.

"D-D-don't you think we sh-sh-should know each other's n-n-names first?"

The kitten rolled around, "Fiiiine, what's your name?"

"I'm Nyke, what's your n-n-name?"

The kitten got to its feet and touched noses with him.

"Kefi, I'm Kefi!" she said, and jumped for him, trying to get at his ear.

A lump of emotion rose in his throat as he heard the name, and he looked up toward Dahlia to see her watching the two of them, her green eyes prominent on her thin face. She blinked at him slowly, he returned the gesture and turned back to Kefi.

"A p-p-pleasure to meet you K-k-kefi. Now, c-c-catch me if you c-c-can!"

Kefi chirped in delight as Nyke dashed away and hid behind a piece of driftwood. He waited to pounce, listening for the sound of tiny paws galloping across the sand.

Chapter Thirty-One

Phira

PHIRA HAD STAYED WITH his body. Curled up against the rain as she'd huddled up next to Mikos to keep him warm. Even now she had no idea why she'd done that. Not much from that night made a lot of sense to her.

She'd watched calmly, soaked to the bone, as Barnabus's human materialized out of the sheets of rain. She'd moved then, with one last look at Mikos, his soaked coat making him look so small laying there on the ground. She'd tried to imagine him looking toward her, but watery drops shattering on his open and sightless eyes gave that up for the lie it was.

Gingerly, the human had knelt and scooped Mikos up into her arms. She'd cradled his body with such tenderness that Phira felt a tinge of hope that perhaps he had survived all along, that this human could somehow bring him back.

That's not what happened of course. Phira had shadowed the human all the way to her home and watched silently as she, carrying Mikos, disappeared inside. She'd waited to see if they came back out, but they did not reappear. Eventually head and tail held low, she'd scampered off and wandered aimlessly in her grief.

Days passed, and she wandered, hardly eating, hardly speaking to any others. More and more often she would end up on Miko's windowsill. The one that was part of his home, his favorite perch for watching the quay.

She sat there for hours a day, watching nothing, consumed by her own thoughts. She'd been so proud of him at that last council meeting, even as he'd stood against her trying to address what she'd considered a very real threat to their livelihood on Poros.

They'd become close by accident. He'd been mistakenly left outside by his humans on an extra chili night, slipping out the door unnoticed. He'd come skittishly exploring her hiding place for the night, looking for a place to stay warm.

"Who are you, find somewhere else, this spot is mine!" she'd hissed at him in warning.

He'd looked toward her with such alarm and confusion on his face she had been taken aback.

"Please," he'd said, *"I don't know where else to go. My sleeping spot is closed to me right now. I... I have a very thick coat. I could help keep you warm for the night."*

For some reason, she'd relented, and he'd come in and curled up with his back to her.

That had been the start of it. After that, he would talk to her every time he saw her, treating her as if they had always been friends. She began to seek him out to ask his opinion on certain topics or just to talk. The baseline compassion he expressed for others was completely foreign to her. Even with the human's generosity, you took what you could get or risked getting nothing at all. Despite the council's edicts there were still cats who went hungry.

Mikos was different though, having come from a different existence. Thanks to his humans, he never wanted anything. It made it difficult for him sometimes to understand that the world did not work that way for everyone.

It had been her idea to have him run for a council seat, her influence that had gotten him elected. She'd thought his voice could perhaps soften the council's views in subtle ways. Not change them completely mind you but shift them toward something more communal.

He had done a little of that, but Mikos on the council was not the same Mikos she's come to know. In the face of other council members, he lost his confidence and more often than not defaulted to backing her opinion, her proposals.

Sitting in his favorite spot, eyes closed against the sun's glare, she recalled all the times she'd tried to pull him out of his shell. All the times she tried to goad him into raising his own ideas and sticking with them. It had never worked though, he always acquiesced. Even when she proposed policies she knew he would be opposed to.

Eventually, she'd given up and let the pattern of their interactions take over. She started taking his support for granted. Working on the assumption that he would support her agenda rather than consulting him for his opinion.

That day though, when he'd come in with Hera, full of fury and challenge and an idea. Her heart had soared at seeing him find his voice, even as she took opposition to it. She had been a little chagrined later when she'd found out it had been a parting jibe from Calix that had set him in motion, but that was nothing compared to the pride she'd felt toward him at that moment.

She'd felt his anger toward her too and understood its origin. Their relationship had evolved into one where she took advantage of him, of their friendship, of their closeness, to get the outcomes she wanted. She'd felt shamed by what they had become and had promised herself and him that she would talk things out with him.

"A conversation that can never happen" she thought to herself as she laid her head down on her paws.

That was her life for the moment, days spent sitting on Mikos's windowsill. Her confused mind seeking a resolution that could never come, leaving her lost in grief and pain.

Then one day, some humans began to take notice of her.

She heard something getting closer than normal. She'd opened her eyes to the sight of a human hand thrust in her direction, holding up a small fish. Her eyes followed the length of arm and came to rest on one of the small humans standing there looking directly at her. She looked around, not daring to maintain eye contact. She did not want to move, but she also did not want to challenge this human. They could be dangerous.

The hand with the fish moved closer to her, cautiously she extended her neck and sniffed at the fish, careful not to look at the human. The fish moved closer, startling her. She pulled back, scooted farther away, out of reach of the human. It looked at her for a bit and then, very slowly, set the small fish down on the windowsill a little way in front of her. After setting it down, the small human backed away and climbed up a set of steps situated next to the window and disappeared inside Mikos's home.

Awareness dawned that that had been one of Mikos's humans. She wondered if they missed him, or even knew he was gone.

The smell of the fish reached her, and she moved forward to sniff at it again.

She'd not been eating much at all, not being all that hungry lately, but the smell of that fish reached something deeper. With a small dainty bite, she picked it up and ended up downing the whole thing in a few seconds.

With the fish settling in her stomach, Phira resumed her position on the sill, watching the world pass by without really noticing.

The next day, the small human was back with another fish. The previous day's events replayed themselves out again. Phira was very wary of humans, even as she accepted their food.

Day after day the small human would check on her, once a day, then twice a day.

Sometimes it brought food, others it would simply make noises at her with an outstretched hand, attempting to touch her. She wasn't quite ready for that, but the steady stream of food was bringing her back to her senses. She found herself able to think more clearly, to feel the sorrow at the loss of Mikos, to miss him terribly, but to also turn her mind to other things. To hash out what she'd wanted to say to him, even if his ears would never hear.

Then one day, she let the small human touch her.

What an experience that was.

Sitting there, taking in the sun, seeing a human move toward you, one of their giant paws moving toward your face. She'd seen other humans touch other cats of course, it simply hadn't been something she'd ever allowed.

Still, she had a full belly, she was relaxed and didn't want to move. She closed her eyes and let it happen. She flinched at the first touch to the side of her face right in front of her ear, but it was gentle, barely there even. To her surprise, she reacted to it, pressing her head up against the human paw, using it to massage her head and neck. It kind of felt like being groomed, except human paws were very soft.

Then the human got its claws involved, actively scratching behind her ears. Despite herself Phira was in heaven.

"What sorcery is this?!" she thought to herself. *"How does it know where to scratch?"*

"Mikos of course," she said aloud.

The human, hearing her, began making noises of its own. Quiet calming noises as if it were speaking to her while it scratched her head.

Phira purred and accepted the attention, feeling a connection to Mikos through the touch of this human.

Days passed and their interactions grew closer and closer.

Phira now waited on the windowsill for the human to emerge, then she'd jump down to greet it. She'd taken to making some of its noises back at it. It seemed to like that and made even more noise. Sometimes the human brought food and then left, others it would sit on the steps and let her climb up into its lap.

She was amazed at what it could do with both paws when it had a mind to. No grooming from another cat brought such an encompassing feeling of contentment. The warmth of its lap, the massage of its paws, it gave her a sense of comfort she had never known.

Then a day came when the small human opened the door but did not step out. It stayed standing there, with one of the larger humans, making noises at her.

Phira had no idea what to do.

The small human knelt down and placed some food on the floor on the other side of the threshold. That got their intent across. Cautiously, she moved toward the food. Neck extended, each step taken slowly and with great care. Phira inched her way toward the food while trying to see everything visible within the human home.

She reached the food and ate it quickly. Once done she turned to dash out the door, but the small human's touch stopped her. The kindness calmed her, and she turned her attention back toward the human dwelling. There was so much to take in, she slowly moved deeper into the human abode. Peeking around corners, hiding behind contraptions she had no idea the use of.

At one point she approached a big cushion, sitting on the floor, the unmistakable scent of Mikos reached her.

"This must be one of the places he slept." She said to herself quietly.

Without a second thought she walked onto the cushion and began to roll around on hit. Drinking in the scent of her lost friend, feeling close to him, remembering him, loving him. She felt the odd sensation of sorrowfully wishing he wasn't gone while also experiencing happiness at being able to experience this part of his life. The humans were making noises at each other, eventually the larger one knelt down and touched her, making a noise.

That is when she noticed the door had been closed, she was trapped inside the human dwelling. She couldn't bring herself to care though, she had a piece of Mikos, and she was loath to leave it. She spent the evening sleeping, imagining the warmth of the cushion to be his warmth. At one point the humans showed her two bowls, one had food in it, the other had water.

She ate and drank, and then explored.

There were many doors to this place, many things to explore, but she began to feel uncomfortable, closed in. There was no open sky over her head, and she didn't like that too much.

The humans seemed to be preparing to sleep for the night. She made her way to the door she'd entered through and stood in front of it, hoping it would open. One of the big humans came up and made some noises at her, they almost sounded like a question.

It opened the door for her, and she looked outside, seeing that night had come and Poros was blanketed in darkness. Phira was about to leave when the voice of the smaller human came from behind her.

She turned and saw it crouched down, both paws extended toward her. It clearly wanted her to stay inside. Phira looked back toward the open door once, then turned to the small human and trotted over to it, tail raised high. The small human enveloped her in its arms and stood up, something she'd grown used to from sitting in its lap.

Phira purred and relaxed into its arms as it carried her through a door and into a room with a large cushion big enough for a human. It set her down and climbed up on the cushion itself. It lay on its side and stretched out its paws toward her Phira moved closer to its head, found a spot, and lay herself down.

As she closed her eyes to sleep, Phira realized these humans had taken her in, as they had Mikos.

She decided to accept their invitation, for while she had lived many places, she had never had a home.

Epilogue

THE WORLD SWAYED.

Back and forth. Back and forth.

"Why was it swaying?"

A memory floated before her, she grasped for it.

A shock of cold, clinging to something, something slippery, everything gray and blurry but with pinpoints of light in the distance. White slivers danced upon the water's surface, broken up by raindrops falling home.

"I was in the water"

The dull roar of something, getting louder.

"Coming closer." she remembered.

A nudge, a desperate climb, human voices. They all meshed in her mind, shattered bits of reality trying to piece themselves together into something whole.

"What happened to me?"

Something warm and not unpleasant smelling kept pushing at her whiskers, intruding on her thoughts.

Slowly, she opened her eyes, tried to focus. Darkness slowly resolved itself into a giant black nose, right in her face. Below it, two huge fangs, wet and glistening rested against a soft pink tongue.

"*AJAX!*"

Calix leapt straight up into a backflip as a surge of energy coursed through her body. Landing on all fours she wasted no time bluffing. Lowering her head, ears clamped to her skull, rear end raised in the air, Calix prepared to counter Ajax's inevitable charge with one of her own. To her mind it was the only way she might survive this encounter. She looked toward her adversary and... faltered.

"Huh?"

Not Ajax, but a puppy, was barreling toward her. Front legs leaping forward in unison in that weird gait they all had until they figured out how to use their legs properly. Its face was a portrait of pure puppy joy, mouth open, tongue flopping around in tandem with its ears. It shouted something as it ran.

"Hey Wester! He's awake!"

The scratch thing was about to plow right into her. Calix knew how to deal with puppies though.

"You stop right there!" she hissed fiercely. "I'll rip that nose of yours right off if you come any closer!"

The puppy's eyes widened, and it tried to stop, planting its front feet to halt its momentum. Its hind legs however, had different intentions. Already poised for another surge forward, they went ahead and completed the motion. It was Calix's turn to have her eyes widen as the puppy's rear end flipped up over its body and came down with a thud right on her face.

She sputtered and backpedaled trying to move herself out of range of the thing's tail.

"It's still scratching wagging!" she thought to herself, as the tip of it smacked against her face a few times before she could get herself safely away.

"Eche, Puppies are the worst," Calix said under her breath, as she readied herself to give this presumptuous pup a good thrashing.

A voice from above her broke her concentration.

"Well, that's certainly an inglorious way to be brought up to speed. Please don't abuse Pasha, she is just a puppy after all."

Calix's eyes followed the sound of this new voice. A few tails up, casually resting on a human stool sat a cat she'd never seen before. It occurred to her she had no idea where she was. Looking around she realized she was in a space built for humans. Some things she recognized, like chairs and couches. Others were completely foreign to her but seemed mostly decorative. Not two tails in front of her, Pasha was sitting, alternating between bashful and curious looks.

"You're on a yacht. Some of the crew were returning last night in the rain and you climbed aboard their zodiac, soaking wet, completely exhausted and half drowned."

"Zodiac?"

"Oh um, a small boat the humans use to get back and forth from land to this yacht. I have to say, I am curious how a cat got himself..."

"Herself."

"...apologies, how a cat got herself into the harbor in the middle of the night during a rainstorm."

"It's a long story," Calix said, "are we still in the harbor?" She'd never hoped for anything more than she hoped they were still in the harbor.

"Unfortunately, we are not." the cat said. "I'm Westminster Tabby by the way. Although Pasha here has gifted me with the name Wester. You may use that, for brevity, if you prefer. I'd say it's a pleasure to meet you, but judging from the way your expression just sunk, I'd say pleasantries aren't really a concern for you right now."

"Calix," she managed to say.

"I'm Pasha!" said the puppy, lifting up both its paws like it was about to jump toward her.

"Dooonn't" Calix said.

Pasha dropped her paws and remained where she was, fidgeting around with barely contained energy. Trying to avoid the reality of her situation Calix's mind focused on an oddity, something Specht had said. She turned to look up at him.

"How do you know what humans name their small boats, Zodiac was it?" she asked.

Wester looked a little surprised she'd asked.

"It's not so much the name of their small boats as it is the name for that specific type of small boat."

Calix leapt up and positioned herself on a stool next to the one Specht was sitting on. Her tail thumped against the stool's cushioned top in annoyance. She stared intently at Specht for a moment, ears forward, letting him know she meant business. After a few moments she rephrased her question.

"And how do you know the human name for a specific type of small boat?"

"Oh THAT?" Wester broke eye contact and looked away, glancing down at Pasha, who'd gotten bored and was currently gnawing on her front paw. "That is also a long story, but the short version is, I can understand some of the human's speech. I'm a scholar."

Calix stared at this Westminster Tabby for a long time, unmoving, deciding if she wanted to believe him or not. She'd never heard of such a thing. There were so many other things she wanted, needed, to ask about, but this revelation captured her imagination and would not let go. She glanced down and Pasha, who seemed to be falling asleep, a paw still in her mouth.

She thought of Nyke, and a pang of sorrow reached out for her.

"Oh Nyke, I wish you were here" she thought to herself.

She knew, though, what Nyke would say if presented with what she'd just heard.

"I'm thinking on this one," she said, still focused on Pasha, "I'd like to hear the long version, if you wouldn't mind."

Acknowledgements

I would like to start of thanking my wife Nidie. Without your wanderlust and passion for travel taking us to places all over the globe I would never found myself in the situations that inspired the story for this book. Without your skills and attention to detail I may have never been able to bring this book to print in any organized way. Without your quiet support I never would have attempted to begin writing at all.

I'm eternally grateful to my mother, father and step father, all of whom continually believed in me, even when I didn't believe in myself.

To Steven Specht, without your mentorship and friendship I would have never made it to this point. Your critique, advice and proof ready was invaluable in helping a collection of rough drafts come together and become a story.

To Missa, thank you so much, you know.

Finally I would like to thank everyone who followed and interacted with my facebook page as I experimented with posting draft chapters. Your feedback, support, and requests for more often kept me going through times when I had considered throwing in the towel and giving up.

About the Author:

He likes cats.

Printed in Great Britain
by Amazon

23985010R00099